OUTER CRYO WORLDS

OUTER CRYO WORLDS

IGOR SHOLOIKO

Copyright © 2021 Igor Sholoiko

The moral right of the author has been asserted.

Apart from any fair dealing for the purposes of research or private study, or criticism or review, as permitted under the Copyright, Designs and Patents Act 1988, this publication may only be reproduced, stored or transmitted, in any form or by any means, with the prior permission in writing of the publishers, or in the case of reprographic reproduction in accordance with the terms of licences issued by the Copyright Licensing Agency. Enquiries concerning reproduction outside those terms should be sent to the publishers.

Matador
9 Priory Business Park,
Wistow Road, Kibworth Beauchamp,
Leicestershire. LE8 0RX
Tel: 0116 279 2299
Email: books@troubador.co.uk
Web: www.troubador.co.uk/matador
Twitter: @matadorbooks

ISBN 978 1 8004 6518 3

British Library Cataloguing in Publication Data.
A catalogue record for this book is available from the British Library.

Printed and bound in the UK by TJ Books Limited, Padstow, Cornwall
Typeset in 11pt Minion Pro by Troubador Publishing Ltd, Leicester, UK

Matador is an imprint of Troubador Publishing Ltd

To explorers of imaginary worlds

INTRODUCTION

Have you ever experienced a nice, enjoyable thought that you return to again and again every time you relax with a G&T in the warmth of the Mediterranean sunshine? I have! Paradoxically, in such situations my mind drifts to snowy Siberian planes, gigantic icebergs in the Arctic Ocean, Antarctic valleys full of penguins, and after a few minutes inevitably reaches the frost of outer space.

Why? Probably because it nicely combines the two subjects that I have been fascinated with for my entire life: low temperatures and celestial bodies.

My fascination with low temperatures started many years ago. Just after my university graduation, I became a junior cryogenic engineer in the Verkin Institute in Kharkov, Ukraine. The first thing which ignited my abnormal interest in "cold" stuff was unlimited access to liquid nitrogen combined with limited access to certain pieces of scientific equipment. Driven by curiosity, I tirelessly stuck different objects into liquid nitrogen and observed the changes caused by the cold. These observations never failed my expectations. Liquid nitrogen made rose petals fragile, as if they were made of glass. Apples became as solid as rocks. My enthusiasm reached a climax once I attempted to produce dry cottage cheese by the cryo-sublimation process. At the time my main hobby was mountaineering, which often took me to remote Asian mountains. During these expeditions, we used to carry all the gear and food we needed in backpacks. Once I learnt about sublimation, I had a eureka moment. If we could freeze cottage cheese using liquid nitrogen, and then keep it in a vacuum, we could take all the water out without destroying its nutritional qualities (as I believed then), reducing the weight of the final product to a third of freshly made cottage cheese. So, one would need to just add water to the sublimated product to make a delicious breakfast, even high up in near-deserted mountains. Back then, it sounded like an unbelievable luxury. Part of me also hoped that I could impress my mountaineering comrades with this genius idea.

I had everything I needed in the lab: a sealed vessel, a vacuum pump and a dewar of liquid nitrogen. After cooling the cheese layered onto a specially made whatnot-like structure and loading it into the vacuum chamber, I left it on the pump running overnight.

The first thing I learnt the next morning was that, yes, I successfully produced about a hundred grams of a granulated substance, which could be turned into edible cottage cheese by adding water. The second piece of news wasn't nearly as exciting. I was told that my boss was looking for me and he was not in a good mood at all… With sweaty palms, I knocked on the door to his office. Here, I need to add that I was extremely lucky, because all my bosses have had great people management skills. My boss then, Yuri Zakharovich, who was my mentor, teacher and introducer to the marvellous world of low temperature physics, was a very wise and exceptionally patient person.

The first thing I heard from him after entering his office was that the pump I used for my small project was dead, because the oil in the pump sucked in water. The oil needed changing. The second thing, to my complete embarrassment, was that I could have stopped the water vapour penetrating the pump. All I needed was a nitrogen cooled trap. The "punishment" for my bad behaviour was changing the pump oil under the supervision of my boss which, actually, gave me a lot of joy. It also gave me a few large stains on my trousers. This stopped me from mass dry cottage cheese production, but didn't deter my interest in liquid nitrogen, which eventually led me to observe a cryo-volcano eruption demonstrated for me by my micro-boss Rebel. I will return to this thrilling story later on.

In all honesty, I don't remember exactly when my fascination with outer space began. It must have been there since I started to understand the surrounding world. As a typical Soviet child born in the early sixties, at the peak of the space exploration enthusiasm, most of my dreams were related to space-travel and outer space worlds. In the sixties and seventies, space exploration was developing so fast that almost all boys and girls dreamed of becoming space-explorers. In the eighties the space race slowed down considerably; by the late eighties I had already settled into my profession as a low temperature physicist and cryogenic engineer. By that time, my interest in outer worlds migrated from inspiration to my imagination, which continued to be fuelled by various discoveries. The first one that blew my mind was the colour photographs of the ground of Venus sent by the Venera 13 spacecraft in 1981. At first glance, the Venera 13 landing site appears quite dull – smooth but broken terrain topped by abundant debris of various sizes. However, in combination with other bits of information such as the incredibly high pressure of 93 bar (approximately 93 times the atmospheric pressure on Earth!), a temperature of 740 K (467°C, 872°F) and the presence of opaque clouds made of sulphuric acid, the colour photographs provided more than enough to fuel my imagination. There was, however, one significant obstacle which prevented me from indulging in the mental modelling of the Venus world. There, a human, even in the most sophisticated space suit, would not survive outside of a spaceship even for a few minutes.

This obstacle completely disappeared in the case of Mars. High resolution images of Martian terrain were obtained by robotic rovers sent to Mars at the beginning of the 21st century. From what we know now, the Martian environment allows for the presence of humans for an almost unlimited time period, as long as they are in specially designed suits. Later, I am going to discuss a DIY Martian space suit, which, I hope, could allow for nice hour-long Martian walks. I actually disagree with the widespread opinion that Mars is a rather boring and inhospitable place for a walk and will try to explain why I think so in the chapter dedicated to Mars.

The final boost, or rather super-boost, to my imagination was the Huygens probe landing on Titan on January 14th,

2005 and sending images of the alien world of this mysterious Saturn satellite to Earth. It turns out that Titan is the only other known body in our Solar system which has rivers, lakes, rain and seasons, but with one striking difference. Instead of water, the role of liquid is played by a mixture of methane and ethane which exists in a liquid state at a temperature of around 100 K (-173°C, -280°F).

You may notice that, so far, I've been using three different temperature scales. It would make sense to select just one, but it's not an easy choice to make, as each of them has an advantage and purpose, which I'd like to explain to you. Before I start, I need to overcome a hurdle psychological in nature. I believe when people talk about subjects of personal passion, it is quite common for them to go into so much detail, turning potentially interesting conversations into lengthy monologues which deter listeners. It worries me that this could happen here. To avoid that risk, I am taking all the lengthy explanations out from the main text and placing them into the *Parallel Thoughts Appendixes* at the end of each chapter. This way, readers won't need to deviate from the main line of the story with me but could always find these long and potentially boring details if they wish to do so.

Now, equipped with this tool I am going to indulge myself with a comprehensive review of all temperature scales. Conceptually, temperature is a degree of heat present in an object and can be measured by a thermometer. We intuitively assign higher or lower temperatures to hot or cold objects respectively and where the concerned temperatures are not extreme, the temperature can be perceived by touch. In all cases, temperature is traditionally defined by a comparative scale. Nowadays there are three most common temperature scales: Fahrenheit (°F), Celsius (°C) and Kelvin (K). All of them evolved as a result of complicated historic processes that involved some of the finest human minds and left behind a few fascinating tales, which I would really like to share with you. Please find them in the *Parallel Thought 0.1*.

Now it is time to explain the prefix "cryo" – a combining form which indicates low temperature in words like cryogenic or cryostat. In the word "cryo-world", which I used in the title of this book, cryo implies that all outer worlds mentioned here have predominantly cryogenic environments. The meaning of the word "cryogenic" might not be that popular in mainstream language, so it makes sense to define it in terms of temperature. According to a patriarch of British cryogenics, Prof Ralph Scurlock[1], cryogenics is the branch of science and technology which deals with the production and effects of temperatures below 250 K or -23°C (i.e. colder than the refrigeration and air-conditioning working temperature range) down to the lowest attainable temperatures approaching absolute zero at 0 K or -273.15°C. This temperature range is most conveniently covered by the Kelvin scale, so let's make that our scale of choice from now on. However, occasionally, I am going to give (in brackets) the temperature in centigrade, just to emphasise how cold it is in comparison with the standard for comfortable human warmth which, according to the World Health Organization, is 18 ± 2°C for healthy adults who are appropriately dressed.

The reason for my anomalous interest in cryo-worlds could be explained by their strangeness and essential unlikeness to the world in which we live. At cryogenic temperatures, the

---

1   Ralph G. Scurlock, *History and Origins of Cryogenics*, Oxford University Press (1993)

properties of materials change dramatically, and ordinary items may behave oddly and counter-intuitively. There are also a few natural phenomena like superconductivity or superfluidity that can take place predominantly at cryogenic temperatures and would have been considered science fiction just over a hundred years ago. If a cryogenic world is not weird enough in itself, we could easily add another level of strangeness by moving it to one of the outer celestial bodies. There, the mixture of cryogenic temperatures, lower gravity and exotic atmospheric conditions could create bizarre realities, which we are going to explore here using knowledge available today, combined with the power of our imagination.

In order to facilitate our fantasy journey, I need to loosen up some of the strict borders of scientific knowledge and let imagination fill the logical gaps. By doing so, I may put myself in dangerous situations of stretching some suggestions beyond what may be considered reasonable, for which I would like to apologise unreservedly.

Here, we are going to discuss the hypothetical possibility of swimming in the liquid methane of Titan's lake using specially designed swimsuits. We will consider the possibility of humans flying on Titan by flapping wings attached to their arms. We will also discuss climbing and skiing in Pluto's mountains which, to a certain extent, is similar to such activities on Earth, except in a space suit and at much lower gravity. I will try to answer the question of why you might find yourself in serious trouble if you try to do the same on Titan's methane glaciers and snowfields. We will pop a champagne bottle on the summit of Olympus Mons – the highest mountain on Mars and probably in the entire solar system. We will also undertake imaginary journeys to observe spectacular cryovolcano eruption on a comet and to explore the deep waters of Europa moon's ocean. Last but not least, we will reflect on the possibility of life on outer cryoworlds, and how it might look if it were to exist.

PARALLEL THOUGHT 0.1
TEMPERATURE AND TEMPERATURE SCALE

As it often happens, the earliest description of a device capable of showing changes in temperature was mentioned in the book *On Nature* written by the ancient Greek philosopher Empedocles of Agrigentum in 460 BC. This family of devices, also known as thermoscopes, could indicate only relative changes in temperature. Later on, after the addition of a scale, the thermoscope evolved into the modern thermometer.

Thermoscopes used during the Hellenic period were mostly based on the pneumatic principle, when heating or cooling led to expansion or contraction of trapped gas respectively. Much later, during the Italian Renaissance, a few inventors, including Galileo Galilei, offered their versions of thermostats. It is thought that Galileo Galilei discovered the specific principle on which the device is based and built the earliest version of Renaissance thermoscopes. Interestingly, one of the most popular thermoscopes of the Renaissance period – the "Galilean thermometer" – was invented not by Galileo himself, but by a group of academics and technicians that included Galileo's pupil, Torricelli, and Torricelli's pupil, Viviani.

Rapid development in technology and science in Post-Renaissance Europe created urgent demand in quantitative temperature measurement. It is not surprising that the English genius Isaac Newton paid his precious attention to this area of science and created one of the first practical empirical temperature scales. He defined zero degrees on his scale as the temperature of melting ice or snow and the 33-degree point as the temperature of boiling water. From this point of view his scale is similar to the Celsius scale but with each Newton degree equating to 100/33 degrees Celsius (°C) and with the same zero temperature point. However, the practicality of the Newton scale significantly loses to that of Celsius due to a large number of reference points (18 points in total), with quite a few having vague descriptions. My favourite reference point is 17 Newton degrees (52°C) that corresponds to "the greatest heat of a bath which one can endure for some time when the hand is dipped in and is kept still". Not very precise, is it?

The next major development happened just over twenty years later, when German physicist Daniel Gabriel Fahrenheit introduced his version of a temperature scale. I have to confess, I cannot understand why the Fahrenheit scale has become so popular that the whole population of the United States uses it daily. Stranger still, the popularity of the Fahrenheit scale sharply declines at U.S. borders. Beyond them, it is almost unknown. The most reasonable explanation would be that the Fahrenheit scale was the first reasonably practical temperature scale that became popular during the peak of European immigration to the New World. The Celsius scale, most popular in today's world, was introduced twenty years later and by the time it gained its popularity in Europe, the Fahrenheit scale had already taken root in the culture of the young American nation.

The improved practicality of the Fahrenheit scale comes from a reduced complexity in comparison with the Newton scale. There are just three important temperature reference points. The lowest reference point, 0°F (-17.8°C), was established as the melting temperature of a solution of brine made from mixture of ammonium salt, water and ice. There was gossip that Fahrenheit actually chose the lowest air temperature measured in his hometown Danzig in the winter as 0°F and only later on found a brine solution which, if mixed with ice, provided a reproducible zero temperature reference point. As the second point Fahrenheit chose the human body's temperature, 96°F (37°C), and the third was defined as the boiling temperature of water at 212°F (100°C).

The next scale introduced by Swedish astronomer Andres Celsius almost twenty years later became the most widespread temperature scale in human history. Today it is used by more than 95% of the world's population. The extraordinary success of this scale can be explained with three primary reasons. First is the scale's simplicity; it is based on just two reference points which are reliably reproducible and well known to the general public. The Celsius zero temperature 0°C is fixed at the freezing point of water and 100°C is the boiling point of water at atmospheric pressure. The second reason is that the Celsius scale is a temperature interval system but not a heat energy ratio system. This means that it follows a relative scale linked to ordinary life experience but not an absolute scale that requires formal scientific definition. Thirdly, the Celsius scale is based on properties of liquid water: the fundamental component of life as we know it. Below 0°C and above 100°C (outside the temperature range of water in a liquid state) organic life becomes extremely difficult, if at all possible.

In 1848, British engineer and scientist William Thomson, also known as Lord Kelvin, proposed an absolute thermometric scale, which we know today as the Kelvin scale. The idea for the Kelvin scale was sparked by the 19th century discovery of a relationship between volume and temperature of a gas. Kelvin found that the volume of a gas should become zero at −273°C and defined this temperature point as an infinite cold or absolute zero. Each unit on this scale is equal to one degree of Celsius but called a Kelvin rather than a degree. According to the Kelvin scale, the absolute zero is 0 K; ice melting point is 273.15 K; and the boiling point of water is 373.15 K.

The choice of the absolute zero point makes the Kelvin scale naturally convenient for a description of the low temperature range and the scale of choice for cryogenic engineers and low temperature physicists. For example, the boiling point of liquid air is around 79 K or -194.35°C; the boiling point of helium at one atmosphere is 4.2 K or -269°C and superfluid transition in liquid helium (below which helium behaves like a fluid with zero viscosity) happens at 2.17 K or -271°C, or -456°F.

Before I conclude **Parallel Thought 0.1** I would like to give you couple simple conversion formulae:

Kelvin into degrees Celsius (°C) :
   T[°C] = T[K] − 273.15

Kelvin into degrees Fahrenheit (°F) :
   T[°F] = (T[K] − 273.15) · 9/5 + 32

ONE
TITAN

Any subject of which we have some knowledge, but without enough detail to form a definitive picture in our minds, provides powerful fuel for the imagination. This is exactly what fuelled my imagination of Titan, not only the largest moon of Saturn, but a personal favourite destination for journeys of my imagination.

I first learned of Titan in my teenage years, when I read Kurt Vonnegut's sci-fi epic, *The Sirens of Titan*. The gigantic, lonely statue of a scientist standing in Titan's frozen desert stuck in my mind and my fascination with this planet-like moon has steadily grown since. So, one can only imagine how euphoric I was when, in 2005, the Huygens probe finally touched down on Titan. Sadly, the statue was not there, but the Huygens team made a few astonishing discoveries, such as huge hydrocarbon lakes and clouds that produce methane rain. In fact, Titan is the only other place in the solar system, besides Earth, that has stable liquid on its surface. Today, there is a consensus amongst the scientific community that methane's role on Titan is quite similar to the role water plays in Earth's hydrological cycle: causing rain and snow, eroding riverbanks and creating methane clouds. This is only possible because of the extremely low temperature on Titan's surface 94 K (-179 C°), resulting from its enormous distance from the Sun; Titan receives about 1% of the amount of sunlight Earth does.

The very high density of Titan's atmosphere (with a pressure 1.45 times higher than that of Earth, and the Moon-like gravity of just $1/7^{th}$ of Earth) completely changes the paradigm of transportation on Titan. The unique combination of these conditions offers the most efficient propulsion for any vehicle. According to the basic aerodynamic model, the propeller's drag force is proportional to the density of fluid, which in the case of Titan's atmosphere is more than four times higher than Earth's. Hence, on Titan, a propeller geometrically similar to those we use here can achieve a drag force a few times larger than on Earth. The same applies to the lift force of airplane wings or helicopter rotors. In combination with low gravity, all these components should be more compact and significantly more energy efficient.

Such a fortunate combination of Titan's environmental conditions could turn one of the oldest human dreams of flying like a bird into reality. The first thought that comes to mind in association with this dream is the ancient Greek myth about Icarus, the son of Daedalus, the creator of the Labyrinth. Icarus, together with his father, attempted to fly away from Crete using wings made by Daedalus, who, by the way, was the most acclaimed craftsman of the Athenian kingdom (Greek mythology was formed far before Athens' democracy). In essence, this is a sad story about a young man's giddiness and an old man's love for his son. A story that ends in the tragic death of Icarus who dropped like a stone from the sky into the sea.

A few years ago, an expert in aerodynamics, Professor Mark Drela from Massachusetts Institute of Technology, concluded that it is simply not possible for humans to fly by flapping their arms with wings attached. According to him, "The arms and chest of a human do not have anywhere near enough muscle mass to provide the necessary power. In theory, human legs do have enough strength to do this, but only if the wings' span is large enough — at least 80 feet (24m) or so — and if they also weigh significantly less than a human." Astonishingly, this would not be a problem on Titan!

Much lower gravity reduces the lifting force required for take-off by more than seven times, shrinking the required wingspan to 3.5m as a result. The high density of Titan's atmosphere reduces the wingspan even further, to around one meter. Now human muscle mass becomes more than capable of providing the necessary power to fly. The modern composite materials of technology allow us to make very light wings which could weigh just a few hundred grams. The negative side of Titan's environment is the extreme cold. This means humans would have to wear a protective space suit which modern thermal insulation technology is already capable of providing. The suit needs to be just a few kilos in weight (including the weight of the oxygen supply equipment) and flexible enough to not restrict the movements of human

limbs. In order to stabilise the body in flight, we also need some kind of tail, just like every bird has. I would suggest using a pair of conventional leg fins that do not need to be large due to the high density of Titan's atmosphere.

Now, when we have all we need to enjoy bird-like flight it looks to me like a fantastic idea to initiate the creation of a new sporting activity never suggested on Earth before, like Quidditch, Harry Potter's flying sport. As it usually happens when dreaming up a new sport, it's best to invent the rules in a similar way to already well-established sports. Using the marathon, a long-distance running race, for example, why not introduce the "Icarus" which could be a long-distance flying race on Titan? This wouldn't be an entirely new idea. In 1988, the Greek Olympic cycling champion, Kanellos Kanellopoulos, skimmed over the Aegean Sea from the island of Crete to the island of Santorini in a specially engineered aircraft, Daedalus 88, propelled by pedals. The entire project was sponsored by the MIT Department of Aeronautics and Astronautics. The record-setting flight of 116km took four hours of intense pedalling. Almost a quarter of a century later, the Royal Aeronautical Society of England established the Icarus Cup in order to promote the sport of human-powered flight, with pedals-based aircrafts in mind. To be honest, the pedal-based flight does not feel authentic to me, just as riding a bicycle for 42km doesn't give you the real marathon experience. That is why I think that the real Icarus challenge should ultimately be based on wing flapping rather than pedalling in a cleverly designed aircraft. The only place in the Solar System where this is possible, in principle, is Titan. Therefore, the real Icarus race could be 116 km flight. A 58km flight would be a half-Icarus, like a half-marathon for those who are inexperienced or not fit enough to complete the full 116 km. I believe both distances are doable if you have favourable wind, which could be quite strong on Titan. The only remaining serious issue for Icarus flyers would be the oxygen supply.

Everybody knows of the bulky and heavy high-pressure tanks integrated into astronaut and scuba diver suits. The main purpose of this cumbersome piece of gear is to squeeze in as much oxygen as possible. The only way to achieve this in Earth's ambient environment is to increase the pressure of the gas, but there is a price for that; high-pressure equipment is notoriously heavy and bulky. Luckily, Titan's temperature is just four degrees higher than the boiling temperature of oxygen and the density of liquid oxygen is almost a thousand times higher than the density of its gas phase at room temperature. It is so high, in fact, that a one litre container of liquid oxygen is enough to support the normal breathing of an average human for about 50 hours. At the same time, the container does not need strong walls to sustain internal high pressure or efficient thermal insulation (remember, just four degrees difference!) and, as a result, could be as light as a few hundred grams. By the way, one litre of liquid oxygen would weigh only 1.14 kilograms. So, in the cryogenic world of Titan, the oxygen supply for human breathing during flying or any other activity is not going to be a problem.

It is important to mention here that flying by flapping one's wings is clearly an extreme scenario. All other options of human powered flight are much easier to achieve. On Titan, Daedalus 88 could be used for longer distances with a much shorter wingspan and would not require the fitness of an Olympic champion to power. Furthermore, the helicopter-like Leonardo's flying machine with a helical airscrew is quite feasible on Titan as well.

Talking of human-powered helicopters, recently a team of students and graduates from the University of Toronto built AeroVelo Atlas, the first human powered helicopter aircraft, which in 2013 reached the goal set by the Igor Sikorsky Competition. Their aircraft, with a main rotor diameter of 20.2m, rose above surface level for just a bit more than 3m. On Titan, a similar performance could be achieved with a rotor less than 3m in diameter. What would be other possible means of transportation on Titan? Keeping in mind that this topic may not be everyone's cup of tea, I will go ahead and move this discussion into ***Parallel Thought 1.1.***

It seems that the unique environment of Titan allows us to populate Titan's skies with a great variety of wonderful flying machines. Yet, in my imagination, I rather relish an image of a luxury hotel suspended below hydrogen-filled zeppelin. Not excessively big; think just less than hundred rooms. This hotel could be endlessly levitating above frozen terrane and hydrocarbon lakes and seas. Restaurants and bars could have windows with panoramic views. Just imagine, you are sitting by window with a gin and tonic with a cucumber watching the colossal Saturn with all its rings rising above Titan's horizon. From the surface of Titan, Saturn would appear to fill one-third to one-half of the sky. No doubt, it would be a remarkable spectacle! Here I would like to make one important comment about "Saturn rise." Because Titan is tidally locked in synchronous rotation with Saturn, it permanently shows only one face to the planet. Therefore, if we stay at the same point on its surface, Saturn would always appear in the same position in Titan's sky. The only way to enjoy the Saturn rising spectacle is to move with relatively high speed across Titan's surface. Our flying hotel provides ideal opportunities for this kind of leisure adventure; in Titan's atmosphere, winds can reach speeds of hundreds of kilometres per hour, enough to see a change in Saturn's position in real time. Hotel suites could also have cosy bull's-eye windows that make you feel like as if you are on a luxury cruise ship, but with the alien Titan view instead of boundless oceans outside.

As soon as I mentioned gin and tonic, I took a break, went down to the bar and made myself a glass of the wonderful drink with a few ice cubes and a slice of cucumber. On the way back, when going upstairs I suddenly realised that this activity would not be so simple on Titan. Obviously, due to the very low gravity the surface of a low viscosity liquid (which gin and tonic definitely is) loses its stability and all the disturbances of the liquid surface would get much larger in scale. In other words, to avoid splashing your gin and tonic on your nice new cardigan, you need to keep your glass

far less than half-full. Nearly empty, in fact. The same applies when you make yourself a cup of a tea, but are too generous when it comes to adding milk, a situation familiar to all of us. Even a dozen steps from the office kitchen to your desk could cost you a tea stain. On Titan, however, your cardigan would be relatively safe, as your tea is only splashing at the very bottom of a deep mug.

This does not mean that low gravity is always a bad thing. On Titan, you could make dessert dishes that on Earth would collapse under their own weight. For example, a tall stable gelée tower on Earth can only be made in the shape of the Eiffel Tower. On Titan, the gelée could be anything from the shape of Big Ben to the Gherkin of London. Serving a gelée tower dessert on a plate with built-in LED lights would leave anybody speechless, at least for a few seconds. What about another low-strength food material like ice cream? I would rather stop at this point because we are certainly deviating from our space/cryogenic agenda.

Let's return to our hotel. The most astonishing feature of this hotel I have thought up is a swimming pool with a glass bottom. Imagine swimming in crystal clear water at comfortable room temperature just a few hundred meters above storming methane seas with a chilling -180 C° beyond the glass. Again, we shouldn't forget about the gin-and-tonic-on-Titan effect previously discussed. An enthusiastic jump into the pool could easily throw a large amount of the pool's water up in the air, creating huge waves. One ridiculous jump and the turbulence would take a while to die down. Please think twice before upsetting other swimmers who simply trying to enjoy a tranquil levitation above the lakes of Titan.

Enough about flying; let's talk about the methane lakes. From all we know about Titan, its lakeshores may look strikingly similar to the beaches of the Dead Sea, though you shouldn't let this illusion trick you. The temperature is not 30 degrees Celsius but more than 200 degrees lower. The quiet, pleasant-looking liquid is not warm salty water but a volatile liquid mixture of methane and ethane. The postcard-like image of Titan's beach appealingly invites us to fantasise about swimming in Titan's lakes. This idea is not that crazy and could be quite realistic, if only we could sort out a couple of problems. Firstly, an already familiar one: the thermal insulation from the cryogenic environment could be resolved by modern spacesuit technology, which successfully protects astronauts from the freezing cold of outer space. The other problem, the ability of an object to float on the surface of a liquid, is trickier to solve. According to the famous principle formulated by Archimedes of Syracuse more than 2000 years ago, the upward buoyant force that is exerted on a body submerged in a fluid is equal to the weight of the fluid that the body displaces. Liquid methane is about 2.2 times thinner than pure water. In practise this means that, if we want to float on the surface of a methane lake, our body (together with the swimsuit) should displace 2.2 times a larger volume of liquid methane than it would water. In other words, we would have to be surrounded by hollow space, which increases our volume without significantly raising our weight. This also means that if ships are to be used on Titan's lakes and seas, they need to be much larger than those on Earth. This is particularly important for the design of an unmanned submarine, which is being developed by NASA engineers "to explore the hydrocarbon rich seas of Saturn's moon Titan."

The trivial solution for the second problem would be some kind of an orb: the spherical shell used for zorbing. A conventional orb is a double-sectioned sphere, with one ball inside the other with a layer of air in between. Both are generally made of transparent plastic. Due to the buoyant nature of orbs, zorbing can also be carried out on water, provided the orb is inflated properly and sealed once the rider is inside. "Water walking" using such orbs has become popular in theme parks across the world. However, I have a feeling that in a conventional orb, the hollow space occupied by air is too excessive. Sure, it's a way of optimising the shape of the void inside the swimsuit, but the geometry of a human body is significantly more complex than a sphere. I have some ideas about the design; if you are curious please join me in ***Parallel Thought 1.2*** dedicated to the design of Titan lake swim suits.

Once we have settled on the "Michelin man" swimsuit design in our minds, we can close our eyes and imagine staying

*on one of the Titan lake's beaches. Before descending into the lake, look around. Your eyes should settle on pale-orange soft sand with a few dusky pink pebbles scattered around, with brownish liquid waves breaking just a few meters away. Why brownish? Find out in **Parallel Thought 1.3**.*

Unfortunately, I know very little about lake transparency on Titan, but I can only hope that it is quite transparent. Otherwise, swimming in Titan's lakes would be less than pleasant.

Before immersing yourself, remember the gin-and-tonic effect. If you jump too enthusiastically, you will likely hit the bottom and damage your suit. Instead, you are better off slowly getting to a point where the liquid covers half of your body and then gently changing your position from vertical to horizontal. Once you are floating in the liquid and the disturbance caused by your entrance subsides, you can continue to swim slowly akin to how you might do when snorkelling in a sea on Earth.

In the first few minutes, I would expect us to enjoy the unique experience of swimming in low gravity and low viscosity liquid; the viscosity of liquid methane is almost ten times lower than that of water. This results in a significantly reduced resistance to any movement. The main outcome of these conditions is that the same swimming efforts would produce more thrust. Do not get too excited; energetic accelerating might cause significant disturbance of the liquid surface due to the gin-and-tonic-effect. The low viscosity of Titan lakes' liquid should also make diving much easier. Yet again, I recommend to please be careful. If you dive too energetically, you might, as we already mentioned before, hit the bottom, damaging your "Michelin man" swimsuit, which provides both protection and insulation. Such damage could have serious consequences for the diver encapsulated in the suit. Having finished our short health and safety training, we can go ahead with our actual Titan lake swim.

After spending some time working out an optimal swimming style, we can finally take a deep breath and have a good look around again. What can we expect to see? An alien, unfamiliar world where, in addition to a peculiar brownish colour liquid, we might have different optics due to the variance in light refraction in the liquid methane and ethane mixture. This would in turn affect our ability to estimate the size and distance of objects. A large pebble on the bottom of a Titan lake, for example, may look different to one lying on the bottom of a familiar water reservoir.

Lastly, how long we can enjoy the marvellous experience of swimming in the Titan lakes depends on how soon we get bored. I can understand why; what would you expect from swimming in a reservoir with just a sandy bottom and a few randomly scattered pebbles? Could there be anything else to fuel our imagination? Actually, there could. There is a possibility that in Titan lakes we will find a couple of fascinating objects, making our swimming adventure that much more exciting.

First is an extra-terrestrial life form, which may exist in the cryogenic environment of Titan. To be honest, very little is known about this form other than there is a glimpse of possibility of its existence.

As we all know, liquid water is a necessary condition for life on Earth. However, in the cryogenic environment of outer worlds, life might exist beyond the boundaries of water-based chemistry. Using quite an unorthodox approach, a group of Cornell chemists and astronomers offered a model for life that could thrive in a harsh, cold world, specifically Titan. The most suitable habitat for these enigmatic creatures would be Titan lakes and seas, which could harbour methane-based, oxygen-free cells that metabolize, reproduce and do everything life on Earth does.

In this particular case, I would like to remind you that the less we know about the subject, the more room is left for imagination. Mine, for example, immediately generates images of gigantic glowing jellyfish capable of striking with fierce electrical discharge. I am going to stop right here and use the trick which helped Scheherazade from *One Thousands and One Nights* to survive ordeal and become King Shahryar's wife. If you, highly respectful reader of this book, are eager to hear the conclusion of this tale, postpone our discussion until the Chapter 4 dedicated to life in outer cryogenic worlds.

Another of the fascinating objects would be a methane iceberg floating on the surface of a Titan lake. Intuitively, it is obvious that solid methane should sink in hydrocarbon liquid, because the solid methane is heavier than the liquid. Nevertheless, some time ago, Jason Hofgartner and Jonathan Lunine from Cornell University suggested that this is not necessarily the case. They modelled Titan's lakes and seas as methane/ethane/nitrogen systems and the buoyancy of solids in these systems and found that ice could float in methane-rich lakes for all temperatures below the freezing point of pure methane. The reason is that solids in methane-rich systems are less dense than the coexisting liquid. They also found that solids in ethane-rich systems require air porosities of greater than approximately 5% in order to float. Interestingly, according to their model, in the case of ethane-rich seas, if the ice forms with an air-filled porosity of between 5% and 10%, the ice can initially float. If the temperature drops by just a few degrees, the ice might sink. This sensitive dependence of the ice behaviour on temperature could lead to some interesting effects. For example, if the surface temperature of the sea oscillates around the point where the solid and liquid have equal density, the lake could actually form ice that both floats and sinks.

By the way, the ability to float might have significant effects on the appearance of methane ice. Depending on the level of air porosity, the methane ice could appear either completely transparent at zero porosity or quite opaque if the porosity is higher than 5%. That means that floating methane ice could look more or less like a conventional water iceberg, which is not that exciting. This lack of excitement could be awesomely compensated by a bizarre bottom ice, known as an anchor ice in Earth's waters, where it is quite rare. Anchor ice has a very bad reputation among hydraulic engineers because its presence can seriously disrupt hydro-electric power plants by reducing their flow or even stopping turbines completely. However, Titan and Earth anchor ice would look different. The Earth's one resembles a piece of sponge or wadding; the Titan ice may look like a thick layer of glass cover on the bottom. If we glance straight down when floating above this ice on the surface of the lake, we might completely miss its presence. If we look further forward, the anchor ice might reveal itself as a mirror-like surface. For example, if we have another swimmer 20 to 30 meters in front of us (say the lake is a few meters deep), we would hardly be able to see this person in horizontal view due to obstruction by surface disturbances. However, we could clearly observe an image of the swimmer reflected from the surface of the methane anchor ice in front of us. This reflection may be similar to an external reflection from a quiet water surface; the only difference is that the reflection comes not from the surface, but from the bottom of the lake. Weird, isn't it?

Now that we know more about methane ice, it seems like a good time to allow ourselves to enjoy swimming in a Titan lake surrounded by floating methane icebergs and anchor ices at the bottom, which should be an undoubtedly amazing experience. After some time to enjoy this remarkable sight, we could start to feel the growing temptation to touch the object of interest – a common intuitive reaction to unusual spectacles or illusions – but, in this particular case, a very bad idea. Let me give you a piece of useful advice: never ever touch methane ice on Titan. If you do, you risk getting stuck to its extremely sticky surface, like a fly to flypaper!

According to the results of research described in **Parallel Thought 1.4,** solid methane is very soft and sticky at the temperatures typical for the surface of Saturn's moon. Even closer to the ice's melting point, around 91K, it behaves like an extremely viscous liquid with a viscosity comparable to the andesite lava. Despite the similarity in mechanical properties, these two substances are quite different; lava is screamingly hot, above + 1000 C° (1273K), while solid methane is freezing cold -180 C° (90K). By the way, we are going to return to this interesting analogy later on, in the Chapter 3 dedicated to cryo-volcanism.

Now that I have explained why touching a methane iceberg is a terrible idea, I think I should reveal other consequences of the weird properties of solid methane that could pose a serious threat to us. One of the few discoveries made by the Cassini mission in 2006 was a mountain range measuring 150km long, 30km wide and 1.5km high. This range lies in the southern hemisphere of Titan and is thought to be composed of icy material and covered in methane snow. As I already mentioned, the average temperature on Titan's surface is just three degrees above methane melting temperature. It is not surprising, therefore, that high in the mountains the temperature could drop below the melting point where solid methane starts to behave like a very viscous and sticky substance. Now let us assume that we are on our mountaineering expedition ascending one of Titan's peaks and we've just approached the edge of a methane snowfield or glacier. Following the best mountaineering practices, we should put on crampons, grab hold of ice axes and proceed to the snowfield. Stop! One step onto the methane snowfield and we would get stuck. We'd then need to produce an upward effort of 180kg force (for an average person's shoe size) to free ourselves. And I'm not even talking about crampons or mountain skis. It is very clear that Titan is not a place for mountain ski resorts.

The time has come to talk about the scariest thing about Titan that I have ever been able to imagine: snowstorms. If methane on Titan plays a similar role to the one water plays in Earth's hydrological cycle, it is reasonable to suggest that methane may precipitate on Titan's surface in the form of rain, snow and probably even hail. As the temperature on Titan is never far from melting point, both methane snowflakes and hail balls would be extremely sticky and have a tendency to aggregate on all surfaces, independent of the surface material.

Let's imagine what it would be like if we got caught in the middle of a methane snowstorm on Titan. *Within a few minutes, our spacesuits would be covered with a thick layer of solid methane. What's worse, we would already be strongly glued to the ground, without the ability to move, let alone run away. Within half an hour, we would form a gigantic snowball, or rather a snowdrift the size of a human. The only way to escape from this ordeal would be to just wait until the snowstorm is gone, for sunshine to completely melt the solid methane. My only hope is that we would have enough oxygen to survive.*

Since we already touched on the subject of Titan's storms, we cannot escape discussing another of Titan's unresolved puzzles: do thunderstorms with lightning exist on Titan? Cloud formations in Titan's atmosphere are just like those on Earth, except the "rain" isn't composed of water, but of liquid methane. Hence, it would be reasonable to suggest that the same charge separation should occur there from time to time, producing lightning. However, no lightning has been directly observed by scientific instruments on any of the spacecrafts, including the Voyager missions launched in the 1970s, the Cassini spacecraft or the Huygens atmospheric entry probe. Scientists still have not lost hope of detecting lightning on Titan, but the chances of this discovery are getting bleaker after each mission. This is a real pity because the lack of lightning steals a Titan storm's thunder.

Another subject we cannot avoid discussing in atmospheric precipitation is the possibility of rainbows in Titan's sky. In Earth's sky, a rainbow is caused by reflection, refraction and dispersion of light in water droplets. Rainbows appear in the sky as a colorful arc, which contains all the colors of light spectrum, starting with red on the outer part through to violet on the inner side. In principle, if Titan's atmosphere was transparent enough, we could see a similar effect on liquid methane droplets instead of water. Due to the different refraction coefficient of liquid methane and, possibly, the size of methane droplets, the radius of the rainbow arc might be different, though the sequence of colors would be the same. However, there is one serious obstacle:

the hazy atmosphere of Titan. The haze on Titan is similar to Earth's pollution and made up of the aerosols formed in the moon's upper atmosphere, as we discussed earlier. This haze is quite efficient in adsorbing ultraviolet, but not the infrared light. As a result, the possibility of observing Titan's rainbow in an infrared spectrum might be higher than in visible light. However, I think you would agree with me that constantly wearing infrared goggles just to peek a glimpse of an infrared rainbow in Titan's sky is on the silly side.

Enough about precipitation. When you live in England, discussing precipitation for too long decreases your popularity. It's a good time to switch to another remarkable feature of Titan: its gigantic and mysterious sand dunes. Dune fields are the second most dominant landform on Titan, after the vast desert-like plains. They cover more than one tenth of the moon's surface, stretching over an area of 10 million square kilometers. Having a basic shape similar to the Arabian Desert dunes, the Titan dunes are larger: one to two kilometers wide, hundreds of kilometers long and more than 100m high. However, like the linear dunes on Earth, their size and spacing vary across the moon's surface which could be explained by differences in local environments.

There is, however, one drastic difference between the locations of dune fields on Earth and Titan. On our planet, they are scattered more or less randomly across all of Earth's terrain. In the case of Titan, dune fields are predominantly found in the southern hemisphere. This phenomenon could be explained by the influence that Saturn's orbit has on Titan's seasons. Because Saturn completes its orbit around the sun in around 30 years, each season on Titan lasts for approximately seven years. The small ellipticity of Saturn's orbit makes Titan summers slightly more intense than winters and, as a result, creates a drier environment in the southern hemisphere. It is therefore logical to suggest that, in drier conditions, the sand grains would be transported easier by the wind to make dunes. The fact that Titan's lakes and seas are mostly found in the northern hemisphere supports this presumption.

Another fundamental difference is the material of the sand particles, which are not made of silicates as on Earth, but of solid hydrocarbons, precipitated (even when I try, I can't stop talking about precipitation!) out of Titan's atmosphere with a small presence of water ice flakes. By the way, these are the same hydrocarbons which are responsible for Titan's atmospheric haze. During or after precipitation, they aggregate into grains up to 1mm in size. In a sense, these grains may be similar to plastic microbeads widely used in modern technology and notoriously famous for their devastating effect on the natural environment.

Another possible explanation was recently suggested by researchers from the University of Hawaii at Manoa. According to them the sand particles could be formed as a result of interaction of high-energy galactic cosmic rays with organics on Titan's surface. Interestingly, colors of species produced in chemical reactions driven by cosmic radiation have different shades of brown from dark yellow to pitch black. That would make Titan's dunes looking like dunes in Karakum Desert in Central Asia. The direct translation of Turkmen words *gara gum* is *dark sand*.

We have to keep in mind though, that at cryogenic temperatures the mechanical properties of these particles are quite different. They are as hard and tough as silicate grains of conventional sand. As a result, we could expect similarity in Titan's sand properties and behavior. For us, walking through the dune fields of Titan would be akin to rambling in the Karakum Desert, but with much smaller gravity and a thicker atmosphere. Also, please do not forget that, unlike the Karakum Desert, Titan is freezing cold. This analogy reminds me of a false statement I made earlier, in which I concluded that Titan is definitely not a place for mountain ski resorts. How wrong I was...

In recent years, the board-sport community experienced a rapid growth in the popularity of sandboarding. This extreme sport is similar to snowboarding and involves riding across or down a sand dune while standing on a board. What we already know about Titan's sand dunes allows us to suggest that we could enjoy a similar sporting activity on Titan. Needless to say, the unique combination of low gravity, the size of the dunes and the higher density of the atmosphere could make the whole experience quite exceptional. Of course, the downhill – or down-dune – skiing using conventional mountain skis should be possible as well, but sandboarding seems more promising to me. As discussed earlier, due to the high density of the atmosphere and low gravity, the surface area of a standard snowboard might be enough to sustain reasonably long gliding. For example, starting from the top of a dune with some initial acceleration, we can jump, glide on a board for a while, touch down and continue our trial in a similar style for a relatively long time. Imagine the perspectives this would open up for sandboarding acrobatics!

Though dune sand skiing is not limited to going downhill, cross-country skiing could be even more pleasant, keeping in mind the glorious landscapes of Titan's ergs. The best location to enjoy the magnificent view would be from the top of the highest dune. Once started, our cross-country skiing trail would follow the dune's top. We could keep going like that for tens of kilometres. I would suggest that the most spectacular view would be at dawn or sunset. Can you imagine the almost effortless gliding on sand at the top of the gigantic dune surrounded by the alien landscape of Titan's erg in the fading red-orange light of the setting sun? What an exceptional feeling!

As is usually the case in beautiful places, there is always a darker side. Some hidden dangers are not easy to recognise at first glance, especially if we are fully preoccupied with picturesque views or overwhelmingly pleasant experiences. In the world of Titan dunes, this dark side is a giant sandstorm in the equatorial regions of Saturn's moon, as recently discovered by astronomers analysing the data obtained by the mapping spectrometer installed on the Cassini spacecraft. This discovery makes Titan the third Solar System body, in addition to Earth and Mars, where sandstorms have been observed. The storms were located right over the dune fields around Titan's equator. Results of computer modelling also suggested that this feature could be a relatively thin layer of tiny airborne solid organic particles, situated just above the moon's surface. The near-surface wind required to elevate this amount of dust would have to be a few times stronger than the average wind speeds estimated by the Huygens measurements near the surface and with climate models. Keeping this in mind, I suggest that Titan's sandstorm may be quite unpleasant, if not dangerous; the windage area of a human body together with sand-board or skis in combination with Titan's low gravity could be enough for this wind to blow us away. Another worrying consequence of a sandstorm could be a very poor visibility. I guess that spinning in a turbulent flow without the ability to see could make us disorientated very easily: circumstances ideal for a panic attack. All that being said, here's my advice: please do not forget to check the local weather report before leaving to enjoy sandboarding or cross-country sand skiing in Titan's ergs. Seriously, at least look out of the window. If you see clouds of dark brownish colour, a sandstorm might be coming.

So far, we have mostly been talking about Titan's spectacular landscapes, bizarre natural phenomena and mind-blowing opportunities for various extreme sport activities. We have not touched on the possible practical reasons of how and why the human civilisation would benefit from exploring and colonising this weird world. The obvious idea of using Titan to mine precious metals and minerals (which may or may not be present on Titan) is not quite realistic because of the remoteness of Saturn's largest moon in the solar system. As an alternative, I would like to offer you an interesting application that came to me in one of my Titan daydreaming sessions. The idea is based on a unique combination of cryogenic temperatures and high-density atmosphere, which is ideal for a moon-size supercomputing facility of the future. Let me explain why in **Parallel Thought 1.5**.

If supercomputing facilities on Titan ever became a reality, they would require a small army of programmers, engineers and support personnel. I strongly believe that, despite the rapid development in artificial intelligence, human involvement in technology will be still required for generations to come. In the case of Titan, it is particularly important because of the communication and logistical problems caused by the enormous distance between our planet and Titan; radio signal travels from Earth to Saturn in about 75 minutes! Though I have no idea how many people would be required to operate this futuristic facility, based on what we know about similar contemporary facilities, I'd estimate a few hundred, at least.

The most challenging problem is how to get all these people and their equipment to Titan in the first place. This is going to be quite a long space journey; it has taken seven years from its launch for spaceship Cassini to get to the entry of Saturn's orbit. I hope that space technology will be capable of speeding up this process in the future but, realistically, it'll never be faster than a few years. Despite this, there is a possibility to make the travel *feel* faster for astronauts by immersing them into a hibernation state. We will discuss this astonishing possibility in detail in **Parallel Thought 4.1** (Chapter 4 "A Frozen Life").

Once we get over the difficult trans-planet journey and finally step onto Titan's soil, we could be generously rewarded with the opportunities offered to us by Titan's unique environment. Now we can fly like Icarus, swim in liquid methane lakes in a "Michelin man" swimsuit, and enjoy Titan dune sandboarding. Real thrill seekers can even chase a methane snowstorm down Titan mountains! Let's please remember our main duty, which is to support the supercomputer operations and maintenance. We can enjoy these marvellous activities in our leisure time once our professional responsibilities are successfully fulfilled. I have a feeling that I am about to run out of steam on the

Titan subject, so just before we leave this marvellous world, we should take a long last look on what would be the future supercomputer facility on Titan. All this in our imagination, of course.

What could we see from the driver's seat of a flying vehicle on Titan? *Whitish columns of methane vapour rising in the sky from chimneys sticking out from the roofs of futuristic buildings. That would be the supercomputer facility, placed near a methane lake. The vapour plumes are leaning due to the wind shift. Long pipes, which look like gigantic spider legs, suck in the liquid methane from the lake. The whole construction is surrounded by an enormous wind turbine farm; their slowly rotating blades in constant motion. A colossal hotel emerges from a group of pale orange clouds a few kilometres away, looking like it could be dirigible. Several car-size flying vehicles, similar to the one we are sitting in, rush in between the supercomputer building and the flying hotel. The glorious Saturn, with its rings and moons hanging in the sky above this pale orange, hazy world...* While it is not that easy to stop the contemplation of such tranquil scenery, it is time to switch to the next destination of our fantasy journey and say goodbye to beautifully strange world of Titan. We are not completely done, however; I am going to return to specific Titan-related matters in following chapters.

PARALLEL THOUGHT 1.1
TRANSPORTATION ON TITAN

Thanks to all the unique features of Titan's environment already discussed, the most viable option for me would be a hoover car propelled by electric fans. Today, global high-tech giants and smaller start-ups compete hard to develop electric, drone-like vehicles for individual transportation. A hoover car based on electric fan propulsion is decisively taking the lead in this race. Take the BlackFly vehicle, for example, developed by flying car start-up Opener and backed by Google co-founder Larry Page. Could you just imagine how superb its performance would be once boosted by the incredible efficiency of propeller-based propulsion on Titan?

It is no surprise that NASA engineers are considering using an eight-rotor drone, Dragonfly, for visiting some locations on Titan to investigate chemistry that could lead to life. According to the mission team, the Dragonfly could explore more than 175km, which is nearly twice the distance that has been travelled up until now by all Mars rovers combined. Like a real dragonfly, the drone could fly from one place to another, collecting and analysing samples of interest.

The fortunate combination of a high-density atmosphere and low gravity is not the only advantage given to transportation technology by Titan's environment. Another one is the extreme cold of this alien world. Here on Earth, transport usually utilises energy released during burning fuel (a fuel oxidation chemical reaction). Oxygen is a gas and the easiest way to store enough of it is to get it pressurised. Wait a moment, haven't we been here before when discussing the oxygen supply for flying athlete participants of the Icarus challenge? If I remember correctly, we found an elegant solution to this problem: storing oxygen in its liquid form.

What about the fuel itself? As it always happens in this world, all positive things have negative sides to them. At Titan's chilling temperatures, all petroleum fuels exist only in a solid state, and it would take significant energy and engineering efforts to keep them liquid. The obvious alternatives are methane, ethane and possibly hydrogen. There is, however, a problem with the last one; hydrogen has significantly lower boiling temperature (by another 60 degrees) than the average temperature on Titan, making it more demanding in terms of storage, transfer and transportation. The easiest solution seems to be a liquid mixture of methane and ethane. Luckily, there is plenty of this stuff on Titan. We just need to scoop up some liquid from the nearest lake and pour it into the fuel tank.

Using oxygen-methane as a binary fuel gives another advantage; it is almost as efficient for running fuel cells as the conventional combination of oxygen/hydrogen. The fuel cell then supplies electricity to electrical motors, which could also benefit from the cryogenic environment of Titan. The temperature on Titan is just 15 degrees above the temperature of operation of commercial high temperature superconductors, also known as HTS. When flowing through HTS wires, the electrical current experiences no resistance and, as a result, has no losses. That makes HTS-based electro-motors more efficient and compact. From a cryogenic engineering point of view, this 15 degrees is a really easy task, but if we want to avoid even the tiniest of complications, we can use wires made of high purity copper. When copper is cooled from Earth's to Titan's temperatures, its electrical resistance drops at least by the order of magnitude. Similarly, the consequence is more efficient and compact electro-motors.

One last question to answer before we hop into the imaginary driver's seat of our flying hoover car: how do we get enough oxygen to run all the transportation vehicles on Saturn's biggest moon? The answer is quite trivial: from water. Water is surprisingly abundant on Titan because its surface is mostly made of water ice. The only thing we need is energy to split water into oxygen and hydrogen and we are lucky to be on Titan again. Then, we can get as much energy as we need thanks to Titan's unique atmospheric conditions. One of the discoveries made by the Huygens probe was that atmosphere was moving around the moon faster than the moon was rotating, a physical characteristic known as superrotation and previously observed on Venus. In other words, Titan is quite a windy place. Luckily, we already know how to harvest energy from wind here on Earth. One of the largest wind farms in the world, the London Array wind offshore farm located 20km off the Kent coast, generates 630 MW of electric power by its 175 turbines. Thanks to the higher density of atmosphere and high speed of wind, a similar wind farm on Titan could easily generate 10x more energy. That is already comparable with the net capacity of a large nuclear power station. If we also take into account all the cryogenic engineering tricks discussed above, plus much lower gravity, we can safely assume that using similar turbines on Titan is much less technically challenging than on Earth.

Now, when we produce enough oxygen by electrochemically splitting water, what should we do with the enormous amount of hydrogen as a by-product? Should we get rid of hydrogen? Is it useless? Of course not! Hydrogen is the perfect candidate to be used as a filling gas in aerostat aircrafts, which might be much more efficient on Titan than on Earth. The reason for that is the dramatic difference between densities of nitrogen gas, the main component of Titan's atmosphere and hydrogen gas at Titan's temperatures. One hydrogen-filled balloon can lift up a mass almost five times higher than a similar balloon can lift on Earth. Just think about the marvellous perspectives opened for using this in airship technology.

Let us take as an example iconic German aircraft Graf Zeppelin. The lifting capacity of an airship with a similar volume of hydrogen gas on Titan could be around 500 Tonnes! In my opinion, this is enough to build a small version of Laputa, an island city that floats in the sky, envisioned by the brilliant Jonathan Swift in his novel *Gulliver's Travels*. If we want a realistic medieval market town with a population of a few hundred inhabitants, we might need to increase the size of the airship, which shouldn't be a problem even for modern technology.

I suspect that as soon as I mentioned a Zeppelin filled with hydrogen gas you might instantly sense danger, which is not surprising. Subconsciously, this type of airship is always associated with the Hindenburg disaster. What is going to happen if our flying hotel gets struck by lightning during one of Titan's thunderstorms? Let me reassure you that there is actually no reason to worry because Titan's atmosphere consists of 98.4% nitrogen with the remaining 1.6% composed mostly of methane (1.4%) and hydrogen (0.1 – 0.2%). There is almost no oxygen in the atmosphere. As a result, hydrogen is a non-flammable gas in Titan's atmosphere, making hydrogen-filled airships completely safe there.

PARALLEL THOUGHT 1.2

DESIGN OF A SUIT FOR SWIMMING IN TITAN LAKES

Luckily, to measure the volume of a human body we do not need high-tech gadgets like computerised laser scanners. The answer can be found following the famous Archimedes "Eureka!" approach, known for more than two thousand years.

Let's fill a bathtub – big enough to accommodate our whole body – with water up to the edge. To achieve that, we need to cover the overflow drain hole with a piece of sticky tape. Once this is filled, let's get into the bathtub and completely submerge under water. The immediate consequence of that would be water overflowing onto the bathroom floor. Once we get our head out of water, we can exclaim "Eureka!" in order to pay a tribute to the genius ancient Greek philosopher. If you don't feel like it, you don't need to exclaim "Eureka!" because the exclamation doesn't influence the results of our measurement. The next thing we need is to collect all the water from the floor and weigh it. Water density is almost one kilogram per litre volume, so now we know the volume (in litres) of the body which enjoyed a quick bath just a few moments ago. If we divide the body weight by this volume, we can obtain a density of the body of interest. A much easier way to find this information is to Google it, assuming that information obtained on the internet is trustworthy. All this to find that the average density of the human body is around 985 kg/m^3. We can reduce the average density of the human body even further to 945 kg/m^3 by maximum inhalation of air. The density of fresh water is 997 kg/m³. That allows us humans to float relatively comfortably on the water's surface. By the way, the typical density of seawater (about 1020 kg/m³) further improves our buoyancy. Remember those photos of tourists floating on their backs in the Dead Sea while reading a book? This is the most spectacular demonstration of the higher density of extremely salty water.

Congratulations! We just successfully accomplished the first step to imagine a suit for swimming in Titan's lakes. However, by ignoring the shape of the human body during our first step, we only delayed facing the same problem in step two: the estimation of the optimal void in the suit's volume. To solve this puzzle, I would like to offer my simplified model of a human body that surprisingly agrees quite well with the volume of my body obtained by the "Eureka!" approach. My model consists of six elements:

- Sphere: head
- Cylinder: torso
- Two cylinders: hands
- Two cylinders: legs

Taking the measurements of these elements is quite similar to taking measurements for tailoring. For example, you may need just one measurement for head (its perimeter) and two for a hand (perimeter around the elbow and length of hand from the shoulder to the end of the middle finger). From perimeters, we can obtain diameters of sphere and cylinders and then calculate the total volume of the model body. Amazingly, in my case the volume obtained from this model differs from the one obtained by "Eureka!" approach by just about 10%. This level of accuracy is more than enough for completing our second step.

Of course, I am not as slim as I was in my twenties, but most of my body parameters are more or less similar to the average human body of a middle-aged male. I did try to encourage my wife to measure her body volume using Archimedes' "Eureka!" approach for building an average female body volume model, but she categorically declined, probably because she is anything but ordinary or average. Due to the absence of a female model, we are left with only one option: to design just the male version of the swimsuit based on me as an average person model. If we want me to be able to swim in liquid methane dressed in a swimsuit, the total volume of me in the swimsuit should be increased by at least a factor of 2.5 in comparison with the volume of my bare body. Also, this should be achieved without significant additional weight associated with the suit. Based on this model, I have done a simple geometrical calculation. If we provide a 5cm air-filled gap between the skin of the human body and the inflatable swimsuit's sheath along the whole body surface, we could reduce weight/volume ratio to the point of sustainable buoyancy in liquid methane. Look at me in this marvellous swimsuit! Does it remind you of anything you've seen before? In this suit I look exactly like the "Michelin man", the symbol of the Michelin tyre company! The inflated nature of this suit could make hand and leg movement more difficult, which could influence our swimming style. In fact, I can see only one realistic option: using leg fins to propel ourselves through the liquid and hand fins or paddles mostly for navigating.

PARALLEL THOUGHT 1.3
WHY LIQUID METHANE IN TITAN LAKES IS BROWNISH

This feature of my fantasy is based on an anecdotal story I heard from my acquaintance who was working for the Joint Institute for Nuclear Research in Dubna, Russia. According to him, many years ago Dubna's scientists were studying the behaviour of methane in neutron radiation. Once the experiment was completed, the scientists decided to wash out the experimental vessel. The vessel was filled with a solvent and vigorously shaken. The liquid was then poured into a glass container. The liquid in the container looked exactly like VSOP cognac. The reason for this familiar colour, according to my acquaintance, was the organic compounds produced from methane by radiolysis, the chemical reactions caused by exposure to radiation.

In Titan's upper atmosphere, the nitrogen and methane under the space radiation generate a thick haze of organic aerosols. Eventually these organic compounds are thought to precipitate to the surface and be dissolved in the methane/ethane liquid of Titan's lakes. That is what gives the liquid a similar brownish-yellow colour.

PARALLEL THOUGHT 1.4
STICKY SOLID METHANE

This story began some time ago in the Rutherford Appleton Laboratory in the UK. There, a group of engineers and scientists had decided to design a new neutron moderator, a device for transforming hot neutrons into the cool ones used in neutron-scattering instruments. This is a very popular tool in science and technology. Because solid methane is known as an efficient material for cooling hot neutrons, the decision has been made to utilise this property in the design of the moderator under consideration. However, at an early stage of moderator modelling and designing, this group of engineers and scientists realised that very little is known about some of the important mechanical properties of solid methane. The literature available at the time was not particularly helpful. A decision was made to measure these properties experimentally in order to come to a conclusion.

Two properties of solid methane were considered as the most important for the moderator design:

1. Adhesion: the ability of one material to stick to another
2. Plasticity: the quality of being easily shaped or moulded

The test results have fascinated researchers. At higher temperatures – from 50 K almost to melting point (around 91 K) – solid methane is soft and sticky. Closer to the melting point its behaviour becomes similar to the behaviour of a very viscous and still sticky liquid. Below 40 K solid methane loses its stickiness and ductility and behaves more or less like normal glass. In a sense, solid methane resembles unsettled epoxy glue at higher temperatures and well polymerised epoxy at lower temperatures. Another unexpected outcome of the measurements was that solid methane sticks in a similar way to different kinds of materials such as aluminium, stainless steel and even PTFE, one of the least sticky materials of all.

PARALLEL THOUGHT 1.5

SUPERCOMPUTING FACILITY ON TITAN

The introduction of electronics-based calculating devices in the middle of the twentieth century marked the definite transition to an era of computer technology. Since then, this technology has been developing at a remarkable rate; from 1956 to 2015, the computing performance has experienced a one trillion-fold increase. This trend shows no signs of stopping in the near future. By now, computer technology has penetrated almost all areas of human activity and even managed to change the basic essence of some. For example, the modern bunking sector cannot exist without computers or communication technology, which is itself one of the incarnations of computer technology. This process will only accelerate in the near future, generating further demand for faster, more powerful computing. In the development of new products, future industries will increasingly rely on computer designing and modelling. Future logistics and production will be entirely operated and controlled by computers. I am not even touching on the subject of artificial intelligence; at the moment, we have no idea of AI's potential impact on the human civilisation.

All the spheres of computer technology mentioned above (and many others) require gargantuan computing power. Today, this power is provided by supercomputers or other large computing facilities that all share the same problem: the excessive heat generated by their servers. One side of this problem is purely economic; for an elite supercomputer, which consumes many megawatts of power, the cost of electricity to run and cool the system is as high as a few million dollars per year. Another side is that the heat generated by a system may also reduce the lifetime of components and significantly affect its reliability. Over the years, there have been diverse approaches to heat management, from pumping liquid coolant through the system, to a hybrid liquid-air cooling system or air-cooling with conventional air conditioning. In all cases, the efficiency of the system ultimately depends on local climate conditions.

As often happens in a free market economy, the optimal solution for this problem has been found by representatives of the most flexible and risk-taking computer-based businesses: digital currency mining. Companies have decided to move their computing facilities to polar countries where they can take advantage of cheaper energy and lower temperatures to power and cool their servers. For some time, Iceland has been Europe's most popular location for miners of digital currencies such as Bitcoin and Ethereum. Recently, some cryptocurrency miners started migrating to Norway and Sweden. In Norway, hydropower accounts for over 99% of electricity production, while in Sweden the number is about 40% with a similar level for nuclear power. Consequently, the price of electricity in these countries does not depend much on fluctuations of fossil fuel prices in world markets and always remains on the lower end. At the same time, the average yearly temperature in Norway is around 1.5°C. When we compare this to a 10.7°C average in France, Norway clearly has a significant advantage, making server cooling simpler and more efficient in northern Europe.

What if the average yearly temperature is lower not by

nine but by 190 degrees compared to France? And what if the atmosphere is also denser? If we want to achieve a higher cooling efficiency, we could use liquid methane/ethane mixture from Titan's lakes as a coolant. Just drop a pipe into the lake and pump the liquid through the computer server, exhausting vapour into the atmosphere.

What if we, like one of the main characters of Dan Brown's *Origin*, would like to use a quantum computer in combination with conventional one? Turns out this is easier on Titan as well! The powerful dilution refrigerator based on the pulsed tube cryo-cooler (normally used for keeping a quantum computer just few milliKelvin above absolute zero) consumes more than 10 kilowatt of electric power. This power is largely spent to keep the whole system below 100K, so this energy could be easily saved if we operate the quantum computer on Titan.

It seems to me that we are doing quite well so far, but what about a cheap and plenteous source of electric power on Titan? As it has being discussed earlier, thanks to the windy weather and dense atmosphere on Titan, wind farms could generate a lot of energy with relatively small investment required for building infrastructure and maintaining the electricity generating equipment. Needless to say, this is a renewable source of energy with minimal impact on the Titan's environment.

TWO

MARS

Mars has always possessed a special place in the human culture. It was assigned a divine status because of its eerie reddish colour and its exclusive position in the morning sky, just before sun rise. These mystifying observations might be the reasons behind this planet being named after the ancient Roman god of war. In my 'celestial body popularity contest' (disclaimer: the contest happens solely in my mind; please treat its results as highly arguable), Mars is in second place after Titan. However, if we consider Mars' place in the science fiction genre, no other celestial body comes close to its popularity. This exclusive celebrity status may be explained by Mars' optimal distance from our planet and highly transparent atmosphere, sometimes obscured by Martian dust storms. The distance from Earth to Mars is not as small as from Earth to the Moon, which makes our natural satellite almost naked, unable to hide even the tiniest detail from observation, but not too distant either. Generations of pre-space era astronomers could observe some major elements of Martian landscape, but could not clearly characterise them, always leaving significant space for human imagination. For instance, 19th century Italian astronomer, Giovanni Schiaparelli, observed linear structures on Mars' surface that he called "canali", mistranslated into English as canals, which led to a belief that they were built by intelligent beings on Mars. The assumption was further heated up by odd announcements made independently by Nikola Tesla and Guglielmo Marconi that their stations had picked up possible radio-communication signals from Mars.

Since the Mariner 4 spacecraft Mars flyby in 1965 the situation has changed dramatically. The on-board camera made and sent back to Earth the first close-up image of the Martian surface. After that, a significant part of Martian mystery quickly evaporated, but in return, it gave a precious effect of presence, which for some people, including myself, provided even stronger fuel for imagination.

My fascination with Mars was further boosted by high-resolution images of Martian surface sent by the robotic rovers Curiosity, Spirit and Opportunity in the early 21st century. Although Spirit and Opportunity are not operational anymore – one got trapped in a sand dune and the other froze to death during a massive dust storm – they were considered the most successful interplanetary NASA missions. Curiosity still explores Martian terrain and continues to send us its marvellous images.

Now, thanks to Elon Musk's entrepreneurial genius, the return of interplanetary human space flights to the agenda of space exploration has radically reduced the remaining distance between my dreams and the reality. The main strategic ambition of the SpaceX Company, founded by Musk, is to get people to Mars in the next couple of decades. To prove the seriousness of its intention, in February 2018 SpaceX launched its Falcon Heavy Rocket towards Mars' orbit. The rocket carried Musk's own cherry-red Tesla roadster with a mannequin driver called "Starman," a nod to David Bowie. SpaceX is also planning the first launch of their super heavy-lift launch vehicle, Starship, in 2021. This mammoth rocket was designed with manned interplanetary missions in mind.

Elon Musk is not alone in his endeavour to get people to Mars within the life spans of today's human population. NASA is also planning Exploration Mission 2, slated for launch as soon as the 2020s. This mission will carry real humans into deep space in Orion capsule on the Space Launch System: an American super heavy-lift launch vehicle. This mission will be an important milestone for NASA's deep space exploration plans that also include a crewed mission to Mars tentatively scheduled in the mid-thirties of this century.

I have to admit that I find this subject so fascinating that I could easily spend hours talking about it. For the sake of keeping in line with the cryogenic agenda of this book, let's continue this discussion in ***Parallel Thought 2.1***.

Let's take it back to basics: what do we actually know about Mars? Mars is the fourth planet from the Sun. It is also the second-smallest planet in the Solar System after Mercury. Mars' radius is almost two times (1.88 to be more precise) smaller than Earth's. This makes Mars' surface gravity 2.6 times smaller than Earth's.

Fascinatingly, this difference can significantly change the dynamics of human movement on Mars. Consequently, the essence and rules of some sports which involve jumping (e.g. basketball, volleyball and other athletic disciplines) should be reviewed. If you are interested in exploring this subject in more detail, I invite you to join me in **Parallel Thought 2.2**.

The second most important difference between Mars and our home planet is the 'coldness' of Mars. Due to Mars' thin atmosphere and distance from the Sun, the surface temperature range expands from a really cryogenic value of 133K (-140°C) during winter in the polar zones to temperatures as high as 293K (20°C) in equatorial summer. For the most part of the Martian year, and in most territories, the temperature stays below the melting point of carbon dioxide, which is good news for outdoor ice rink activities discussed in **Parallel Thought 2.2**. As a result, most carbon dioxide and water can exist on Mars either as a solid or as a cold, low pressure gas. When I say low pressure, I mean *really low*; the average Martian surface pressure is about 0.6% of the atmospheric pressure on Earth. Exceptions to this are the low-lying areas of the planet, particularly in the Hellas Planitia impact basin. This basin is so deep that the atmospheric pressure at the bottom reaches 12% of Earth's. So, if the temperature exceeded 0°C, liquid water could exist there.

I'm afraid that everything said about Mars so far might create an impression that Martian terrain is just a barren, frozen desert where there are no exciting things to do and no interesting places to visit. This fits with the common opinion that Mars is a boring place; personally, I disagree. I ask that you give me a chance to convince you that this world is the opposite of boring.

I am going to revert to what I call a quick virtual personality change technique, an idea I borrowed from an ancient Japanese theatre tradition, Noh. I am going to put on a travel agent's mask to virtually transform myself into a space travel agent who is trying to convince you that Mars is a beautiful place to go on vacation. Of course, my presentation of Mars' attractions might be a little exaggerated, but what would you expect from a travel agent eager to sell you an imaginary "mar(s)vellous travel package"?

Let me introduce you to the trip of a lifetime, one you simply cannot miss. This is your chance to be one of the first people to visit Olympus Mons, the highest mountain in the Solar System! At 24km high, it is three times the height of Mt Everest. Unlike Everest, it stands alone in a beautiful conical shape, with grace akin to Mt Fuji. Unobstructed by other interfering mountain ranges, and more than six times grander than the peak of the Land of the Rising Sun, you can truly appreciate the greatness of this colossal mountain.

If you choose our "New Year: Sunrise on the Peak" package, you can watch the sun come up from over 400kms away, with the first rays lighting up a beautiful landscape, with a size equivalent to Ireland. If you are still thinking of visiting Mt Fuji instead, let me put it into perspective: that's double what you would see, and you don't have to deal with typical New Year's crowds.

Alternatively, you could simply take our "Beautiful Views Package"! On Mars you could enjoy Olympus Mons' view from around 350km, whereas on a crisp winter day on Earth, Mt Fuji can be seen only from central Tokyo, about 100km away. In more familiar terms, you can see as far a distance between Mt Fuji and Sendai! In a scale more common for Europeans, this is approximately the distance between London and Paris. If you're American, think the distance between New York and Washington. Using the power of our imaginations and positioning Olympus Mons near Washington, we may expect that tourists on a Hudson River boat trip could enjoy a view of the Statue of Liberty with colossal Olympus Mons in the background.

You can enjoy the magnificent view from such a long distance thanks to the transparency of Mars' quiet atmosphere, caused by a much smaller density of gas which results in a reduced ability to sustain dust particles and tiny water droplets, snowflakes or ice particles, floating in the surrounding air.

In some rare cases, this view might be obstructed by Martian dust storms. Don't worry if you get caught in one. Martian storms are mild; due to the thin atmosphere, you can't be blown away by wind, nor can the storm tilt launch vehicles or affect metal satellite dishes. The winds on the Red Planet are also less than half the speed of some hurricane-force winds on Earth.

I'd like to remove my Noh mask and indulge in a dream about the imaginary ascent of Olympus Mons. I know I am not alone in this; social media has buzzed with this idea for some time. Obvious obstacles in this endeavour include cryogenic temperatures, lack of oxygen in Martian atmosphere and higher levels of radiation on Mars. This last problem is not as serious; as we discussed in **Parallel Thought 2.1**, the radiation dose received whilst staying on Mars' surface is lower than that of the International Space Station. Luckily, modern spacesuit technology is ready to provide light and efficient individual gear for a space-mountaineer to enjoy hours of non-stop climbing. I would like to expand on this subject and offer you my thoughts on a DIY suit to survive on Mars. If this subject is of any interest to you, stick around for **Parallel Thought 2.3**.

In addition, there are some oxygen and other logistical supplies problems, but they could be resolved by an expedition-style mountaineering project. This would imply teamwork; even in lower gravity, it would be impossible for an individual to carry that amount of weight. Secondly, this approach to organised ascent assumes setting up a number of camps stocked up on food and supplies that consist of one (or a few) tents, depending on the stage and scale of the expedition. As soon as I mentioned the word "tent" I descended into my favourite area of contemplation, one of my idées fixes. I could spend hours thinking about the would-be-design and technology behind the Martian mountaineering tent. For climbers, mountaineers, walkers and all other active travellers, a tent symbolises shelter and sanctuary and, in more practical terms, a place to hide from the harsh environment and have a comfortable rest after a day's worth of intense activities. Imagine coming to the end of a day full of ghastly wind, sleet and cold rain. Completely exhausted, you want one thing: to take off your damp clothes and get into a soft, warm sleeping bag. Is there a more pleasant feeling? If you're particularly interested in Martian tent design, I invite you to **Parallel Thought 2.4**.

Now that the virtual tent is in our rucksack, let's imagine that we are about to set up the tent after a long, exhausting day of climbing. There is actually not that much to do. First, we need to find an even, flat space, then roll out the tent, get inside it, seal the zip lock, inflate the inner space of the tent with oxygen from a high-pressure bottle, switch on the electric heater built into the upper layer of the mattress and wait for few minutes. Once the pressure and temperature in the tent reach a comfortable level, we can take off the breathing face mask, oxygen supply kit and heavy mountaineering boots and finally get relaxed and start enjoying the comfort of the tent. Before we give ourselves into the arms of Morpheus, I would suggest making a nice cup of instant coffee. Not tea, unfortunately; the pressure is still too low for that. A warning before you make a cuppa, do NOT use an open flame. In the oxygen atmosphere, your tent could disappear in few seconds. Personally, I'd also prepare a portion of freeze-dried cottage cheese, soaked in water for ten minutes and topped with thin layer of strawberry jam. Yummy! If cottage cheese isn't your thing, you can choose from your preferred array of freeze-dried foods such as mashed potatoes, pesto or even cheesecake.

Many years ago, I actually witnessed the consequences

of a nylon tent catching fire from a camping stove in high mountain windy conditions. We found three shocked fellows sitting in complete silence, each in a sleeping bag in open air, a kettle steaming on the primus stove. Once their emotional shock had gone, we learned that it has taken just a few seconds for the upper part of their tent to disappear after the primus flame touched its nylon wall. Do not forget, this happened in Earth's atmosphere, which contains just 21% oxygen. Can you imagine how fast your tent could disappear if you were to have a similar accident in 100% oxygen? Take my advice and please use only spark-free electrical heaters for making your cup of coffee or preheating your meal. Needless to say, smoking in this tent is also strictly prohibited!

Feeling refreshed after spending a few hours in our tent, it is time to continue our journey to Olympus Mons' summit. I cannot even imagine the strength of emotions a climber would feel once, after days of hard work, he or she finally reaches the summit of the highest mountain in the Solar System. I would expect this person stay happy and speechless for a few moments, looking down over a vast area of Martian terrain and reflecting. Soon after, I suspect there would be an explosion of joy accompanied by an "I did it!" or "Yes!" or just "A-a-a-a-a!".

Unfortunately crying or shouting on Mars isn't as easy as it is on Earth, as your face is covered by an oxygen mask or another, similar device. I have an alternative suggestion; why not celebrate this wonderful event in a more traditional style – commonly accepted for less extraordinary events on Earth – by opening a bottle of champagne. We have to keep in mind though, that this has nothing to do with actual champagne drinking; we simply couldn't do this in a Martian environment unless we had a specially designed retractable liquid sucking device. Think an insect's tube-like mouthparts incorporated into our breathing facemask or helmet. Though this is an interesting idea, let's not deviate from our main aim: celebrating the conquering of Olympus Mons. Why open the champagne at all, then? Because of the spectacular visual effects that would be produced by the jet of sparkling wine escaping from the bottle in low pressure, low temperature environment on the summit of Olympus Mons.

Let's look at the bottle opening process in few steps. First, before we start the process, the bottle should be settled at Earth's room temperature, around 20C°. After loosening the wire cage, let's shake the bottle to stir up the carbonation in order to generate the maximum number of tiny bubbles possible. Then, let's use a thumb to push the cork out from beneath the lip until the cork pops out of the bottle. We might need a pair of flexible gloves to control the process better.

Friedrich Balck of Clausethal Technical University in northwest Germany found that a vigorously shaken bottle of champagne (with a pressure of 2.5 bars) expelled its cork at 40km/h. This speed of ejection would send the cork more than 10m high on Mars. On Earth, it would be much less impressive, just a couple of meters, taking into account the friction in Earth's atmosphere and higher gravity. Nonetheless, it would be better to not aim the bottle directly upwards because when it returns back to yourself, your friends or any breakable items, it would have almost the same velocity as when it left the bottle. Much of the wine will spurt out almost instantly and turn into "diamond dust." Broken into a tiny droplet, the liquid will start to evaporate into the very thin atmosphere, rapidly cooling itself due to evaporation. Within a fraction of a second, all droplets would turn into tiny crystals. At that point, we could finally enjoy a cloud of sparkling, diamond-like particles precipitating to the summit and members of your team. By the way, we don't need to be on top of Olympus Mons to enjoy this "champagne diamond dust" spectacle; a similar show could be performed anywhere on Mars.

It feels like a good time to put the mask of our Noh travel agent back on and present the next point of our destination: the Valles Marineris.

With the Valles Marineris package, you get to experience the Grand Canyon of Mars, a colossal valley extending over 3000km long and spanning as much as 600km wide. That's 75 times bigger than Earth's Grand Canyon, in case you were wondering. If that isn't enough, it delves as much as 8km deep, compared to Earth's puny 1.8km. There is a theory that the canyon started as a crack billions of years ago as the planet cooled. With the true origin of this marvellous wonder unknown, it is shrouded in an aura of mystery. Who knows what lurks beyond?

This package offers the most spectacular way to explore the Valles Marineris: a flight along the canyon on one of our aircrafts. Depending on the option you choose, you can enjoy the grandiosity of the view through large side windows or a glass cabin with transparent walls and floor. You are free to choose the speed of your journey. Even on a faster flight (around 3000km/h), you will have at least a couple of hours to enjoy the scenery.

Though you have the option of a guided tour, I'll be honest, this is not our most popular add-on; the whole geological history of this natural wonder would take a guide no more than ten minutes to present. Instead, I'd recommend reading the brochure beforehand so you can spend your journey focused on the panoramic views of the majestic Canyon in beautiful silence. Some might find the idea of silent observation a little tame. In that case, you could opt to spice up your journey with a Martian wine testing. I know there is no such a thing as Martian wine yet, but we have ambitious plans to offer this option in the future. The unique combination of Martian soil, gravity and spectrum of light could make the flavours and aromas of Martian wines quite unique. Think of the differences we have already seen with New World wines offering distinct aromas and flavours. On Mars, this would be even more remarkable.

Let me paint you a picture and transfer you on-board the flying tour aircraft. You are sitting in a comfortable armchair near huge panoramic windows. The flight started about ten minutes ago and is now in stable autopilot mode. An android, Marty (because he's Martian), in an elegant tuxedo pours you Martian wine, telling you everything there is to know about Martian wine varieties and optimal harvest years in a kind-hearted Stephen Fry voice. Needless to say, the robot knows everything about the Canyon and wine and is ready to answer any of your questions. Listening to the android talk and slowly sipping wine, you can genuinely enjoy the magnificent bird's-eye view of Mars' Grand Canyon. If you prefer, you can simply ask him to listen to what's on your mind or invite him to contemplate the universe in silence with you.

Unfortunately, before we can enjoy a flight over the Red Planet to its full extent, our technology needs to overcome a few technical challenges caused by the very thin and cold Martian atmosphere. To discuss this, alongside other technical challenges of transportation on the Red Planet, I would like to invite you to join me in **Parallel Thought 2.5**.

To travel around the Grand Canyon in a flying aircraft is not the only option we could consider. On Earth, this is not even the most popular mode of travel; jeep tours in the Grand Canyon are far more common than helicopter or airplane excursions. The obvious advantages of this form of travel are that it gives us another perspective on this colossal spectacle and, at the same time, opens up the opportunity to enjoy off-road driving in challenging terrain conditions. On Mars, the travel route could go either through the bottom of the Canyon or along its edge. In the second case I would limit the driving hours to daytime only because of a serious safety issue; dropping from a cliff a few kilometres' high is not a good idea, even in the reduced gravity of Mars. There are also some technical challenges imposed by Martian environment on surface vehicles which I discuss in **Parallel Thought 2.5**. As it follows from the discussion, a reasonable distance for a day trip could be estimated at around 100km. After that, travellers may need a night break in a shelter or luxury hotel, depending on their preferences, where they could rest and sleep, while the vehicle is being refuelled and serviced. This night break could also provide the unique opportunity to experience vivid stargazing in a Martian night sky.

On planet Earth, night stargazing is especially enjoyable in high altitude deserts where cold and dry environments prevent mist formation. This is actually the reason behind the location choices for some of the most advanced optical telescopes, such as the Extremely Large Telescope currently under construction in Atacama Desert of northern Chile and the Thirty Meter Telescope planned to be built on Mauna Kea volcano on the island of Hawaii. Another desirable condition for perfect stargazing would be remoteness from densely populated centres of human civilisation because these areas usually suffer from intense light pollution. Almost all Martian locations satisfy both conditions and, if you allow me a brave futurological prognosis, the situation with anthropogenic light pollutions on Mars is not going to change significantly for quite a while. There are only two known atmospheric phenomena that could spoil stargazing joy: Martian dust storms and a thick haze of light sprinkling snow-like particles observed in Martian polar zones. The last phenomenon is similar to the "diamond dust" that falls from the sky on some cold nights in Earth's Arctic regions, as well as to the "diamond dust" we might expect to observe when opening a bottle of champagne on Mars, as discussed earlier. Fortunately, both phenomena would be rare for stargazing on Mars.

Let's close our eyes and allow a Star Trek-like transporter transfer our minds into a cabin of an 8x8 vehicle that looks like a gigantic Lunokhod. Large windows installed around the perimeter of the vehicle provide a perfect panoramic view over the Grand Canyon of Mars. Our team consists of four members, all of us experienced travellers and very good friends. It is my turn to drive and I am fully focused on the task, manoeuvring between large reddish boulders. During the day we enjoyed a scenic drive and got countless holographic photos of the magnificent Grand Canyon along the way, which have already been posted on Instagram. The intensity of these impressions has emotionally exhausted all of us; everybody, including myself, is looking forward to the night's break. Luckily, we can already make out a strange looking building which consists of interconnected semi-spherical sections resembling a bunch of gigantic mushrooms. According to our satnav, we are just a few hundred meters away from today's destination point: the night shelter. Though the anticipation of our arrival clearly boosts the morale of our team, we still need to get closer, so autopilot can take over and precisely park the vehicle in the designated area near the entrance compartment.

Finally, the vehicle is parked and a telescopic trunk protrudes from the shelter wall towards the vehicle's airlock. The door is sealed and we can hear a hissing sound of air filling the airlock chamber. Both side doors slide off and we walk into the reception of the space hotel. All the rooms in the hotel have a semi-spherical shape, typical for 3D printed buildings, of which there are many on this planet. After taking off our spacesuits and putting them into storage, each of us heads to our own bedroom connected to the main hall by sliding doors. Porthole windows on the ceiling of the main hall and sidewalls of bedrooms fill the building with sunlight creating a bright and open feeling. Though the giant king size bed is undoubtedly the central piece of the bedroom, my attention is fully focused on the power-shower. Quickly taking off all clothes I jump into the power-shower cubicle and give up myself to the beautifully intense hot waterjets, the pleasure noticeably magnified by the thought of how freezing cold it is outside the building, just less than a metre away. After my long hot shower, I dry my body with warm air and choose soft, comfortable clothes in which to join the team gathered in the main hall. Dinner has already been served by Canny the Canyon Robot Chef; everybody is waiting for me to start the feast. For half an hour, we sit and consume the delicious meal in silence. Just before dessert, conversation sparks. With passion, we discuss our thoughts and emotions about the day's trip. There are so many that we could keep on and on and on, but we need to have a rest before we continue the journey tomorrow morning. We polish off the bottle of wine and wish each other goodnight, retreating to our separate rooms.

This is the moment I was waiting for. Once I get comfortable lying on my back in the middle of the king size bed, I give the hotel's robot-porter an instruction: "Open the roof." The roof shutters slip away, opening the glass cupola which covers the upper half of the room. It is already dark, perfect timing for enjoying stargazing to the full extent. For me, the maximum joy of beholding a heaven full of millions of stars could be achieved with Bach's organ prelude f minor playing quietly in the background. When I was a child, I could spend hours looking into the night sky but now, after such intense day, tiredness takes its toll and I fall asleep. Thanks to artificial intelligence, the hotel's management system detects my drowsiness, closes the shutters and lets the music fade out.

I am woken a few hours later, in the earliest hours of the morning; it's still dark outside. All the morning procedures must be completed in time for another remarkable spectacle: the sunrise in the Grand Canyon of Mars. My morning exercise is cut short, not that I mind much.

We manage to get together in the viewing room ten minutes before sunrise. The hotel's robot-chef, Canny, kindly offers us a carafe of hot coffee, which smells so appealing. The side-shutter slips aside revealing a large panoramic window, which, as we've been informed, faces the Grand Canyon cliff. It is still dark outside, but the sky is already illuminated by approaching dawn. The sky gradually gets lighter. Despite everybody expecting it to happen, the moment that a beam of sunlight touches the top of the cliff comes as a complete surprise. The tiny area lit by light is so bright that it is almost painful to look directly at it. The rest of the cliff is still immersed in darkness. As time passes by, the lit area grows, gradually revealing the glorious cliff of Mars' Grand Canyon. The contrast of the view gradually decreases, filling the whole valley with soft orange light. After half an hour of sightseeing, we are invited by Canny into the main hall where breakfast has been served. We eat quickly and, after limited preparation, are back at our vehicle, ready to continue our amazing journey, full of exciting moments ahead.

That seems like enough exploitation for our imaginations; let's turn back to the main storyline and discuss our final destination: the ice-filled Korolev crater.

The crater is named after Sergei Korolev, the chief designer of the Soviet space program that sent the first artificial satellite called Sputnik into space in the 1950s and later made Yuri Gagarin the first human to break into outer space. This magnificent crater is 82km in diameter and located in the northern lowlands of the Red Planet. A detailed picture of the crater has been composed of five strip-like images taken by the European Space Agency's Mars Express Probe. Unlike other impact craters, the rim around the Korolev crater rises high above the surrounded plain, trapping thin Martian air above it. This air pillow acts like an efficient insulator that significantly reduces sublimation of water and carbon dioxide from the ice surface, so water cannot escape from there. In the centre of crater the ice may be a couple of kilometres thick which means that the crater could contain as much water as the Great Bear Lake in northern Canada.

The crater itself – with its flat icy surface surrounded by rocky rim – should be a remarkable spectacle. However, it is the smoothness of its surface that could turn this place into a real Martian wonder. Unfortunately, we do not know for certain how smooth the ice surface is there. If we assume a similarity with frozen lakes here on Earth, it could be smooth enough for ice-skating which opens up incredible opportunities.

Original skates from the Stone Age were made of animal bones strapped to the bottom of the foot. Fast forward to medieval times when the Dutch invented the modern way of skating by introducing steel blades with sharpened edges. The trick is that ice surface is so mechanically strong that it can sustain quite high pressure without significant deformation. The contact between ice and blade is minimal; as a result, the friction force, proportional to the contact area, is also very small. This allows low friction skating, where we can move inertially for a relatively long distance after just one push, due to the blades' sharp edges. Fun fact, the skating blade was an extremely timely invention. At this time, Europe had suffered from the consequences of the Little Ice Age, where all of central and northern European rivers and lakes froze solid during winter. Holland, which was then one of the major trade hubs of medieval Europe, transported almost all in-land goods on barges, which passed through a network of canals. The barges were moved either by working animals like draft horses or by power of wind, if they were equipped with sails. In a sense, skating helped the Dutch to maintain the shipping of goods during the winter season. Once the Little Ice Age ended, this way of transportation lost its popularity and has since been forgotten. However, the individual skating experience was so enjoyable that it later evolved into a number of sporting activities, which remain extremely popular today.

I don't blame you for wondering why I chose to deviate from the main task of showing you the Korolev crater in its best and focused instead on the ice skating. The reason for that is that the unique Martian environment could transform skating on the crater's ice into an unforgettable experience. Firstly, the lower gravity on Mars significantly reduces the friction force between blade and ice, which is proportional to the vertical force caused by the object's weight. Indicative demonstration may be a distance taken by a speed-skating athlete who just crossed the finish line and keeps sliding due to inertia. On Mars, the same athlete moving at the same speed would be expected to stop after more than double the distance. It also means that towing a barge of the same mass on Mars would require much less effort than in a medieval frozen canal. Nevertheless, this is not going to make the life of working animals on Mars easier; for survival and proper functioning in a Martian environment, these animals would need a special protective suit and oxygen supply. Hmm, "space suit for a draft horse." Though this is a nice subject to think about, I feel it's best to return to the main storyline.

Using a sail as propulsion is not an option because Martian atmosphere is too thin for generating a meaningful driving force even in stormy conditions. It seems to me that the best propulsion solution in this situation would be the rocket engine discussed in ***Parallel Thought 2.5***. Rarefaction of Martian atmosphere is not only an obstacle for sailing on Mars, but also an advantage that could increase the speed of skating even further. An aerodynamic friction or drag is proportional to the density of the fluid and the Martian atmosphere is about hundred times thinner than on Earth.

The British jet car, Thrust Super Sonic Car, holds the world land-speed record, set in 1997, when it achieved a speed of 1,228km/h and became the first land vehicle to break the sound barrier. On Mars, a vehicle with similar mass and engine power could easily achieve a higher velocity. The irony of the situation is that the Korolev crater is too small for riding this kind of vehicle; at 3,000km/h it would cross the crater in less than a couple of minutes. A more realistic option for enjoying high speed driving on the Korolev crater would be a smaller, single seater vehicle like a motorbike. The motorcycle speed record of around 600km/h could be easily doubled if not tripled on Mars if we implement a few, relatively simple design changes. First, we would need to replace the two wheels with three blades; by removing the wheels we would also lose the gyroscopic part of the stabilizing force, so three points of contact would help maintain the balance.

We would also need to replace the motorbike's petrol engine with a rocket one. In turn, we'd need tanks for fuel and oxidant. The tanks are not expected to be massive because the requirements for the imaginary ice-jet's engine power are quite modest (due to low aerodynamic resistance and friction), which equates to low fuel consumption. There is, however, a negative consequence of these changes: the three-blade design makes leaning into a turn almost impossible. In combination with an extremely high speed, this will require an enormous increase in the turning radius. Luckily, it is not a problem in the case of the Korolev crater. Even if we suggest a circular racing track with a 50km diameter, it would take just over six minutes to complete one full circle at 1500km/h.

I assume that a Martian ice-jet-skate race would make an enjoyable event for both participants and spectators. The latter could observe a whole racetrack if they were situated at the top of the Korolev crater rim, which rises around 2km above the surroundings. You may argue that following an ice-jet – the size of a motorcycle at a 50km distance – could be very challenging. The jet engine should leave a contrail similar to those produced by aircraft engine exhausts at cruising altitudes. The contrails composed of water ice crystals could be easily seen from tens of kilometres away. In the words of our travel agent, *"It's your chance to experience the spectacle of a lifetime, the fastest and coolest race you've ever seen. You could even try out for the crater ice-jet riding yourself if you dare."*

Apart from the ice-jet race, there are a number of other icy sports one could enjoy in the Korolev crater. These include ice hockey, figure skating and, for those who really like to push themselves to the extreme, ice speed skating around the 250km-long perimeter of the crater's ice lake. Due to reasons discussed above, the speed of a skater on Korolev crater's ice would be considerably higher than the maximum speed achieved on Earth, somewhere around 60km/h. The skater could complete the whole distance in less time than it takes an average marathon runner to whizz through 42km on Earth.

For those who prefer activities unrelated to ice, there may be snow slopes potentially suitable for skiing and snowboarding. I would advise to approach these activities with caution; they could be much quicker than they would be on Earth. If you're an enthusiast of walking and hiking, you could enjoy a spectacular walk along the crater's rim. Beautiful views on both sides of the rim are guaranteed. From there, one can see the whole crater's interior, as well as the vast expanse of surrounding terrain.

My Korolev crater's advertising campaign might be testing your patience by now. I feel that we have managed to almost all interesting aspects of the cryogenic world of Mars except the most important one. Never mind, for it is custom to serve delicious desserts at the end of meals. Before we end the chapter, we must talk about Life on Mars.

For hundreds of years many great minds were convinced that our red neighbour harboured intelligent life forms. A little more than a century ago, this idea has experienced a surge in popularity. One of the fathers of science fiction, the great Herbert Wells, populated Mars with terrifying, intelligent creatures in his novel, *The War of the Worlds*. After exhausting all resources on their native planet, Martians attempted extermination of the human race to claim planet Earth for themselves. Since then, the evil image of ugly octopus-like organisms has deeply stuck in readers' minds. Though the Martians in Ray Bradbury's *The Martian Chronicles* appear more human, these have done little to reduce the level of antipathy towards these extra-terrestrial creatures. It is no surprise, therefore, that Martians become extinct in many sci-fi novels, but nor is the power of an author's imagination responsible for killing the idea of intelligent Martians.

Instead, it was the set of close-look images of the Martian surface sent by Mariner 4 spacecraft back to the Earth in 1965. To explain how, I invite you to have a look at Google Earth or a similar virtual map based on satellite imaging. It is obvious that our human civilisation left many traces which can be easily seen on images taken from a similar distance and with similar resolution as those sent by Mariner 4. I am not even talking about objects of the modern era. Most ancient roads, irrigation systems, fortifications and colossal cult constructions are easily recognisable on the space images, even if they are in a state of ruin. Since the success of the Mariner program, many more images of Martian surface have been delivered by numerous survey missions. Some of them, like the Mars Global Surveyor, achieved extraordinarily high resolutions. None of these images had revealed artefacts similar to those associated with ancient civilisations that are abundant on the virtual maps of Earth. These observations have almost eliminated the chances that intelligent life has ever existed on Mars. However, despite the conclusion being generally accepted by the scientific community, some enthusiasts of alternative systems of knowledge keep spotting mysterious features such as "pyramids" and the "Face on Mars." Later, the Martian photo album has been replenished by images taken by cameras installed on the robotically operated Mars rovers Sojourner, Opportunity, Spirit, and Curiosity. These images gave fresh food for a variety of Martian artefact-spotting enthusiasts who spent sleepless nights meticulously examining images returned by the rovers. On the internet, you can find numerous "fragments of roads," strange looking objects and even ruins of an abandoned fortress found by them. If you ask for my opinion, I would say that to recognise the signs of intelligent life in these images, one needs an extraordinarily powerful imagination and completely atrophied scepticism. Keep in mind that this is just my personal opinion. To put an end to the dispute one needs to send a group of human researchers or extremely advanced robots to Mars, so they can investigate these controversial objects on the spot. Realistically speaking, this is not going to happen in the very near future, so the Martian artefact spotters could continue enjoying their hobby for now.

To be honest, I feel uncomfortable when the power of logic forces me to shrink my imagination. To compensate for this feeling, I'd like to change the focus of the discussion from the native Martian civilisation to the advanced alien civilisations from the outer reaches of the Solar System. The chances of their existence somewhere, not far from our Solar System, are much higher than the chances of there being a native Martian civilisation. In case an alien spaceship visited the Red Planet in the last three billion years, its relics should be well preserved by Martian environment. This is because the most recent geologic era, which lasted on Mars for three billion years, is characterized by low rates of meteorite impacts and by cold, dry conditions, broadly similar to those on Mars today. Another positive argument is that such a long waiting time would make the probability of even a very unlikely event more significant. Who knows, maybe the remains of an alien ship are somewhere on the Martian surface, waiting to be discovered by space archaeologists or astro-archaeologists of the future. Astro-archaeology sounds like a fascinating profession to me. It harmonically combines the adventure of space exploration with the desire to reveal secrets of ancient alien civilisations. Though this profession does not yet exist, it may well emerge in the foreseeable future. In order to fulfil a yin-yang equilibrium, I'd suggest two fictional personifications of an astro-archaeologist: a male version – we'll call him Han Jones – and a female – Indiana Solo. My guess is that we can all picture what Han Jones would look like, but envisioning Indiana Solo may be a more entertaining process. Though I have a picture in my mind, I won't share it with you, as that would rob you from the joy of creating one yourself.

Astro-archaeologists might not yet exist, but astrobiologists do. And though this is a more established profession, it is no less exciting. The idea that microbial forms of life existed on Mars in the past – when it was a more hospitable place – or have even managed to survive until today has been broadly debated in the astrobiology community. There are a number of interesting arguments for and against the microbial life on Mars. We'll get involved in this discussion later on; for now, I'll refer to Scheherazade's trick again and ask you to postpone this discussion until the chapter dedicated to life in outer cryo worlds.

Over the last few paragraphs, I have started to sense a decline in my enthusiasm. If a storyteller loses passion for storytelling, listeners also struggle to sustain interest. It seems a good time to bring this chapter to a close, though I know there are many fascinating topics left uncovered: Martian dust devils, vast dunes, mars-quakes, night sky ultraviolet light pulsing, avalanches near Mars's North Pole, tsunami wind in Hellas Impact Crater, the largest and deepest on the planet and many others.

Such immensity seems impossible to grasp, so I would prefer to leave the Red Planet for now. We may return later on.

PARALLEL THOUGHT 2.1
TRAVEL TO MARS

A transfer to Mars should not take as long as to Titan. According to NASA's "Human Exploration of Mars Design Reference Architecture 5.0," the mission based on Hohmann transfer orbit should consists of a transfer phase from Earth to Mars orbit of about 200 days, a stay on Mars' surface of 400 to 500 days, and a return trip to our home planet of about 200 days. An alternative mission would need about 300 days each way and a stay on Mars of about 40 days. To conclude, the total duration of a crewed Mars mission would be between two and three years.

The overall mission to Mars would require a few cargo transportation missions and the manned lander/ascent vehicle, which would be transported to Mars' orbit, where it would be waiting for the crew's arrival. Then, after assembly of the human transfer vehicle in low Earth orbit, the crew would arrive and the trip to Mars would begin.

The configuration of the habitation module suggests the astronauts/cosmonauts/taikonauts' main living area has general dimensions of 5-6m in diameter and 10m in length. To me, spending 14 months in such a restricted space with other team members seems challenging, both psychologically and physically. As I already mentioned in the "Titan" Chapter 1 and will discuss in detail in **Parallel Thought 4.1** ("A Frozen Life" Chapter 4), it would be nice to spend most of the travel in hibernation state, though I'm afraid that this technology may not be available yet in the short time-scale set up by Elon Musk or NASA. Scientific communities have already tried to address these problems by running mock Mars missions that simulate conditions of space travel and stay on Mars for a few months. The most well-known are the Russian Mars-500 mission and the NASA-funded HI-SEAS program (which stands for Hawaii Space Exploration Analog and Simulation). Both experiments studied some technical and practical aspects of living on Mars, but a large part of the investigation was concentrated on how a group of people live together in isolation with little to no privacy. After concluding the mission, the engineering officer for HI-SEAS, Ansley Barnard, gave valuable advice for future missions: "Remember that the toilet systems are also a system and they're a living system, so stay in balance with those, let them talk to you, if they smell a certain way or act a certain way, they're trying to tell you something, so listen." As you can tell, participants of the mock mission experienced some strange feelings and intense thoughts during their experiment. I hope that, by the time the human mission to Mars is launched, most potential psychosocial problems can be resolved. Such optimism is based on the immense progress achieved by behavioural science in the last decade. Look how efficient high tech corporations have become in selling their products, or how effective political PR companies are at influencing voter preferences. Don't get me wrong, I am not comfortable with either of those examples. What seems much more noble is to exploit the power of a scientific approach to resolve human behaviour problems during space missions.

Up until now, I have managed to avoid the big white elephant in the room – cosmic radiation – which is undoubtedly the biggest threat to human life and wellbeing during a Mars mission. What better time to discuss this important issue in more detail?

It is a well-known fact that at the International Space Station (ISS) astronauts are exposed to hundreds of times more radiation than we are on the ground. Even so, they are to a large extent protected by Earth's magnetosphere and the bulk of the planet, which shields them from Earth's side. Going to Mars means leaving this protected zone of low orbit space. The exposure to radiation during interplanetary spaceflight is more than five times higher than on the ISS. If we multiply the radiation rate by the length of travel and add the radiation dose received whilst staying on Mars' surface (expected to be slightly lower than on the ISS), the total accumulated radiation gets alarmingly close to the critical level for human wellbeing.

Throughout the entire trip, astronauts must be protected from two sources of radiation. The first comes from the sun, which regularly releases a steady stream of solar particles, as well as occasional larger bursts in the wake of giant explosions, such as solar flares and coronal mass ejections. The second source of radiation is galactic cosmic rays: extremely high-energy particles thrown into our solar system either from other stars in the Milky Way or other galaxies. These particles are more energetic, and can knock apart atoms in whatever they strike, like an astronaut (ouch!), or metal walls/other components of a spacecraft. This causes sub-atomic particles to shower into the habitat space. This so-called secondary radiation is particularly dangerous for astronauts. Fortunately, there is a technical solution which can reduce an astronaut's exposure to radiation below dangerous levels. Over the last few decades, the scientific community has actively discussed the possibility of using magnetic shielding of habitable modules from galactic cosmic rays. These studies suggested that, in principle, a toroidal field produced by a superconducting magnet around the habitable module can reduce the dose of a galactic cosmic ray by a factor of ten (at most). It is also worth mentioning that this estimation is based on an "optimistic" theoretical model.

Just a few years ago, an international team of scientists and engineers under the auspices of National Laboratory of Frascati in Italy developed the concept of Active Radiation Shields for Space Exploration Missions. This concept offers feasible design of active magnetic shielding based on intermediate or high temperature superconductors. The use of these novel superconducting wires allows a substantial increase of shielding magnetic field and simplification of the magnet cooling systems, which could then be based on liquid hydrogen, or even liquid nitrogen. This would replace the more complex liquid helium systems required for conventional low temperature superconducting magnets.

The design of the magnetic shield thoroughly modelled in the concept study is capable of reducing the adsorbed dose due to galactic cosmic rays to make acceptable the risk of developing long-term diseases after a return trip to Mars.

Staying for longer in deep space or taking trips farther into the Solar System would require a combination of more advanced passive and active shields, as well as medical treatment that could counteract some (if not all) detrimental health effects caused by radiation exposure.

There is also hope that scientific discoveries of the future may open new opportunities to protect space travellers from radiation. For example, spaceship designers might use the fungus "Cladosporium sphaerospermum" to absorb incoming radiation. This organism has been found near the Chernobyl reactor, and it thrives on nuclear radiation due to radio-synthesis, the process in which melanin is used by the fungus to convert gamma radiation into chemical energy. Recently NASA space scientists grew the fungus inside the ISS for a month and studied its ability to block radiation. After this experiment, there is talk of shielding astronauts and space objects with a layer of this radiation-absorbing protective fungus. Who knows, it may happen that the walls of future spaceships will be covered with fungi... it'll be travelling back in time to the walls of man caves in the Stone Age.

PARALLEL THOUGHT 2.2
SPORTS ON MARS

Mars' surface gravity is 2.6 times smaller than on Earth. That difference should significantly change the dynamics of human movements on Mars. For example, say an athlete makes an ordinary two-foot vertical jump (about 0.6m) on Earth. On Mars the height of a jump with the same physical effort would compare to the height of an average human. Of course, we're talking about indoor activities; the type of spacesuit required for outdoor survival on Mars would make jumping much less enjoyable. To make these games as interesting and competitive as on Earth, on Mars we'd need to raise a basketball hoop or volleyball net by more than 1m. Keep in mind that, on Mars, the flying time of a jump increases, meaning we should also increase the size of the basketball court by a few meters. In volleyball the change could be even more substantial because ballistic ball trajectory is flattened by smaller gravity, also known as Alan Shepard's effect. Apollo astronaut Alan Shepard managed to take a golf ball and club along with him to the Moon, becoming the first person to play golf on another world. He hit the golf ball to travel "for miles and miles and miles." Martian gravity is higher than the Moon's. Combining this gravity with the atmospheric pressure, we can expect the golf ball to travel for hundreds and hundreds of metres, a more modest result, longer than it would travel on Earth, but not as long as it would travel on the Moon. If you are going to the Martian golf course, don't forget to take a golf cart with you, otherwise you are doomed to spend most of the time walking in an uncomfortable Martian space suit.

Let's return to Martian volleyball. In order to let the ball touch the ground or floor inside the opponents' court after the first serve, the court size should be increased by at least 50%. All these changes could slow down the game because players will spend more time flying during a jump. In return, we'd witness bizarre jumps that would make the overall game much more spectacular.

There is an indoor sport game, which is not expected to be significantly affected by the lower gravity on Mars: mini football. The only noticeable difference, I suggest, is that running during the game would require a lot less effort.

Ice hockey is the only outdoor game on Mars which makes sense to me, primarily due to the planet's extremely low temperature. This harsh condition, in combination with very thin atmosphere, makes survival on Mars only possible if a human were to wear a special protective suit complete with oxygen supply. On Earth, the total weight of ice hockey protective equipment can reach up to 7kg. Therefore, if we find a way to combine isolating properties of the Martian suit with protective elements of ice hockey equipment and keep the total gear weight reasonable, we could enjoy this marvellous outdoor game on Mars. An obvious benefit, is how easy it is to create an ice rink on Mars. Just pour water on a flat surface. There is no need for complicated refrigerating equipment to keep water frozen; it is already freezing cold.

The only obvious downside of an outdoor ice rink on Mars could be quick water sublimation from the ice surface; in other words, the evaporation of water molecules from its solid state because of very low atmospheric pressure on Mars. In these circumstances we may need frequent water top ups for maintaining the acceptable ice thickness. But it is clear that water is going to be a valuable commodity on Mars, so using it for this purpose looks like an unacceptable extravaganza. The alternative, more elegant solution is to use solid carbon dioxide instead, as this is the main component of the Martian atmosphere. Known as dry ice, carbon dioxide remains solid below 194K (-78.5°C) which is about 15 degrees lower than Mars' average temperature 210K (-63°C).

PARALLEL THOUGHT 2.3
MARTIAN DIY SPACE SUIT

Why do we actually need a spacesuit to survive in the Martian environment? Most of us will remember the scene in *Total Recall*, when Arnold Schwarzenegger was suffocating on Mars. Those crazy eyes were somewhat exaggerated – it is Hollywood, after all – but the overall picture is not far from the truth. Without a protective suit of some kind, a human being will not survive on Mars for longer than a few minutes.

Why?

1. Absence of oxygen
2. Extremely low temperatures
3. Low pressure of Martian atmosphere

To a certain extent, there is a place on our planet where a similar combination of threats to the human body occurs naturally. I am talking about a 8,848 metre high summit, Everest, where the average temperature is below -30°C and the atmospheric pressure is 1/3 of the pressure at Earth's sea level. A few thousand people have successfully summited Everest, some of them without the use of supplemental oxygen. This fact is useful to help us estimate the level of extreme conditions in which people can survive, at least for a few hours without special protection (though, obviously, these people are equipped with warm clothing and oxygen supply equipment).

The history of aeronautics knows an even more extreme case of exposure to a similar combination of hazards. In

1927, American balloonist Hawthorne Gray reached 13km where the pressure is ten times less than atmospheric and the temperature is as low as −50°C. Gray survived. The aim of his flight was to evaluate the high altitude clothing and oxygen supply equipment available at that time. Needless to say, there was much less of a Health & Safety culture 100 years ago. Nevertheless, thanks to the remarkable fearlessness and curiosity of this man, we obtained unique knowledge about a human surviving in an environment close to a Martian one. For comparison, the average temperature on Mars is −55°C, and its surface pressure is 0.006 of our ambient atmospheric pressure. It is worth mentioning, though, that there are places on Mars (like Hellas Planitia crater) that are so deep that the atmospheric pressure at the bottom reaches the value comparable to the one experienced by Hawthorne Gray during his flight.

The first, very positive outcome of this historic fact is that, at such low pressures, people do *not* burst like soap bubbles. The strength of our skeletons, as well as the elasticity of our muscles and skin are capable of holding the pressure difference between inside and outside of our body. Two parts of our bodies are most vulnerable to the pressure difference: eyes and ears. Yet, they occupy quite a small area, and could be easily covered by a facemask and earplugs. The oxygen supply for breathing is by far the most important for human survival. Luckily, the oxygen supply equipment has been being developed for more than one hundred years. Today, this equipment is efficient and reliable. The only aspect left to sort out is the protection of our body from the cryogenic temperatures of Martian environment. I find this to be the most fascinating topic because it combines a low temperature environment with the extremely low pressure of thin atmosphere and lower gravity. This curious combination of parameters dramatically changes all heat-exchange processes on Mars.

First of all, Martian thin atmosphere is not as sufficient as Earth's when it comes to retaining heat that results in more extreme temperature variations. These variations depend on multiple factors, including location, time of the day and season. I already mentioned that the average temperature on Mars is around 218K (−55°C). However, the surface temperatures may reach as high as 293K (20°C) at noon, at the equator, and as low as 120K (−153°C) at night in the polar zone. Sometimes and in certain places, the temperature difference between day and night can also reach a staggering 100 degrees.

The second important consequence of the low pressure of Martian atmosphere is that it has a dramatic impact on heat transfer. The heat is transferred to and from the human body through three channels of energy exchange: atmospheric gas convection, infrared radiation and thermal conductivity. Thermal conductivity of the still air is negligibly small in comparison with the other two channels. The exchange through the infrared radiation channel is also relatively low in comparison with convection, the dominant channel of the heat transfer between the human body and ambient environment. The convection is the movement caused by the tendency of hotter – and therefore less dense – gas or liquid to rise. Colder, denser material sinks under the influence of gravity, which consequently results in heat transfer. Astonishingly, from all three heat transfer mechanisms, the convection is most affected by the lower pressure of atmosphere and smaller gravity on Mars. Both parameters dramatically reduce the intensity of the convection. This should significantly lower the heat exchange between Martian environment and the human body in both fully dressed and naked forms.

The low pressure of Martian atmosphere could also improve insulating properties of conventional clothing. The main function of any warm clothing is to isolate a person from a cold environment. Usually, this goal is achieved by wrapping a human body in a layer of fabric made from wool, cotton, or a similar fibre. The air trapped between fibres cannot move, which almost completely kills convection, leaving only heat transfer through fibres and trapped gas. The scale of this heat transfer is much smaller than convection would be. The human civilisation has used this approach for thousands of years. Even today, despite mind-blowing successes in material research, traditional clothes remain the dominant way of protecting humans from cold and heat. The low pressure of Martian atmosphere further reduces the conductivity of trapped carbon dioxide gas, the main component of Martian atmosphere, making ordinary clothes even more efficient. Let me put it this way, the military pilot costume of Captain Gray could definitely protect him from the hypothermia on Mars.

It may come as a surprise to find out that standing on Martian surface would make your feet tens of degrees warmer than your head. This is another remarkable consequence of drastically reduced convection in Martian atmosphere.

Last but not least, there is another important consequence of exposure to pressure lower than 20mbar (or 0.02 of our ambient atmospheric pressure). Below this level, the water starts to intensively evaporate from surfaces at room temperature. When water evaporates, energy is removed from the surface, causing a temperature drop. This method, known as a vacuum cooling, is rapidly gaining popularity in the food preservation industry. For example, after leafy vegetables (like salads), are exposed to low pressure, the temperature drops from 20°C to 2°C in less than 20 minutes. Vaccuum cooling can become quite a series hazard, especially when we consider that up to 60% of the human adult body consists of water.

I hope we are well armed now to approach the thought-provoking challenge of designing a DIY suit which would help us survive an hour walk on Mars. Let's start by defining a few basic criteria which would allow us to assess how well the suit of our design is fit for purpose. First of all, our one-hour walk should not irreversibly affect our health or have long lasting consequences for our wellbeing. It's just not worth it. The level of our suffering should not be so high so as to suck all the joy out of our walk (or most of the walk, at least). We should be able to bend down and pick up a small rock or other objects of similar size and weight, inspect them and throw them as far away as possible. It would also be nice to have the chance to try a small jump or short run, just to get the feel of reduced gravity on Mars. If this all sounds fair enough, let's get our hands dirty!

I'd start by wrapping our naked body in cling film to stop water evaporation and prevent vacuum cooling. We should be meticulous, starting from our toes, continuing up our legs, torso and arms, to finish around the top of our necks. I'd also recommend using a pair of latex gloves and a polyethylene shower cap. On top of the layer of cling film, I'd put on thermal underwear and a pair of warm socks.

Despite the conclusion drawn above that the human

body is strong enough to prevent itself from bursting in Martian atmosphere, I would recommend a Lycra speed-skating suit, which should apply some tension on the skin and partly compensate the pressure differential between the inside and outside of the body. This decision would definitely help us feel more comfortable.

The next pieces of clothing are waterproof trousers and a jacket for high-altitude mountaineering. In combination with the two layers already on us, they should provide all the thermal insulation required for our survival. We also have to add a pair of appropriate gloves and mountaineering boots designed for walking on glaciers and fern fields.

The next component of our kit is extremely important; without it we could not survive for longer than a few minutes. Naturally, I am talking about equipment, which supplies oxygen for breathing. We would need a high-pressure oxygen gas bottle with a pressure gage and regulator. Imagine one of those sets used in scuba diving; oxygen could be supplied through the diving face mask. Before we put on the mask, we may need to apply a defog gel to its inside to keep it crystal clear during the walk. The other problem: breathing pure oxygen at reduced pressure may cause symptoms similar to altitude sickness due to the higher rate of water vapour lost from the lungs. Though I don't think an hour walk could result in serious health problems, using a glass bubbler inserted between the oxygen bottle and mask may solve the problem altogether.

Last but not least, to seal the remaining gap between the hood of the speed-skating suit and the mask, I'd suggest wearing a woollen balaclava topped with a Siberian version of ushanka-hat, ear flaps down.

We're ready to enjoy our hour-long walk on Martian terrain. At least I bloody well hope we are.

Let me be clear: I have no doubt that professional spacesuit engineers or designers could do a much better job and provide us with light, flexible, comfortable spacesuits for living and working on Mars. For example, over the past few years, a great deal of progress has been achieved by engineers designing the new generation of Z-series of extra-vehicular activity space suits under NASA's Advanced Exploration System program. The Z-2 prototype suits are being developed for both microgravity and planetary environments. These are expected to make astronauts' lives (both in and out of work) a lot more comfortable, especially during long term missions.

PARALLEL THOUGHT 2.4
DESIGN OF THE MARTIAN TENT

A conventional tent has a few important functions: protecting a human being from freezing conditions, precipitations of different kinds and strong wind. Therefore, it is not surprising that "Himalayan" class tents, designed for extremely harsh environments, are very high-tech. High-tech often means expensive. In this tent, a mountaineer can survive sub-zero temperatures, strong wind, rain, snow and even medium size hail. Remember, though, as we have discussed before, conditions on Mars are far more extreme. Cryogenic temperatures and very low atmospheric pressure (close to no oxygen at all) make Martian environment more similar to the outer space rather than to Antarctic or Himalayan conditions on Earth.

Given that, would it be possible – in principle – to design a tent capable of providing a comfortable environment for a human being to spend a night on Mars?

Let's discuss this fascinating topic in more detail, starting with the low atmospheric pressure on Mars. The lowest pressure in which a human being can survive in natural conditions on Earth occurs on the summit of Mt Everest; this is about 1/3 of the atmospheric pressure at sea level. Funnily enough, this is why you cannot make a decent cup of tea there, as the kettle will boil at just 72°C. Another, slightly more serious consequence is that, at this kind of atmospheric pressure, we'll start gasping for oxygen. That is why most climbers carry a bottle of oxygen during the final stage of their ascent to Mt Everest. Despite all these difficulties, the optimistic conclusion is that a human could not only survive, but have a reasonable level of activity in 1/3 of the atmospheric pressure, for at least a few days.

I might even have an idea how to protect a human from Martian low atmospheric pressure environment. Let's take a simple sealable food plastic bag, blow into it and seal it. For some time, the bag should be fine, without visibly losing shape or internal pressure. Today's self-press resealable zip-lock plastic bags can be found in each supermarket or at the security gates of international airports. What a great example of a clever combination of engineering and advances in material science! Self-pressed zip lock bags can comfortably keep atmospheric pressure outside the bag and almost vacuum inside. In our case we need to keep 1/3 of atmospheric pressure in a gigantic, human-sized sealed bag surrounded by almost vacuum. I'm quite confident that scaling up the zip-lock is a doable task today.

Problem number two: how do we keep a human warm in the extremely low temperatures of Martian environment? Luckily, this problem can easily be resolved thanks to advancements in the modern cryogenic superinsulation (or multilayer insulation) technology. The multilayer insulation was invented around the 1960s for space applications. Since then, it has proved itself to be extremely efficient. Superinsulation generally contains multiple layers of reflective material separated by spacers having low conductivity. There is a snag here: superinsulation works efficiently in high vacuum. In our case, the thermal conductivity of carbon dioxide at low pressure of Martian atmosphere is small enough to provide satisfactory insulation for our purposes. Now, once we have a couple of ideas about how to solve these problems, then we can move onto a possible design. In order to avoid mechanical punctures (potentially caused by sharp stones on Martian soil), I'd suggest an inflatable mattress made of robust material as a floor/bed of the tent. The floor mattress needs to be inflated to a pressure slightly higher than that in the tent in order to form a basement for the entire structure.

You might be thinking this proposed design will increase the weight of the tent. Though you're right, this isn't a problem! Remember, lower gravity more than halves the weight of everything on Mars.

PARALLEL THOUGHT 2.5
TRANSPORTATION ON MARS

The atmospheric conditions near the surface of Mars are similar to those on Earth but at an altitude of around 28km. Aeroplanes propelled by air-breathing jet engines (turbojet, turbofan, etc.) can get as high as 26km. The absolute record is still held by SR71 Blackbird. For comparison, the highest altitude of the iconic supersonic passenger jet, Concord, was 18.3km. This explains why I have estimated our Martian aircraft's speed to be around 3000km/h; the Concord's speed is 2179km/h and the Blackbird's is 3540km/h. From an atmosphere density point of view, the modern air-breathing aircraft technology sits just on the border of what is possible in Martian world. The only option for higher altitude flights on the Red Planet is the rocket technology. While we're on the subject, the British company Reaction Engines is already developing SABRE technology, which aims to combine features of turbojet and rocket engines for propelling both high-speed aircraft and spacecraft on Earth.

There are also two other fundamental differences of the Martian environment. One of these applies significant limitation, but another creates opportunities for aircraft technology on Mars. Let's start from the first, undesirable one. This is a lack of oxygen in Martian atmosphere, which consists of 95.32% carbon dioxide and another 2.7% nitrogen. This lack of oxygen means we cannot use aircraft engines in air-breathing mode; no oxygen means no sustained burning of fuel. As a result, we have to carry all required oxygen on board of the aircraft together with the fuel. This is definitely a drawback for Martian aircraft propulsion. The second distinction is lot more positive. As I've mentioned before, the gravity on the surface of Mars is 2.6 times smaller than on Earth. Which means…the essential power required to lift up an aircraft is 2.6 times smaller on Mars!

A SABRE-like aircraft is not the only option under consideration. NASA engineers have developed a small, autonomous helicopter drone for the agency's upcoming Mars 2020 rover mission. The drone is expected to be less than 1.8kg with a body about the size of a football. The helicopter will attempt to fly up to a few hundred meters, climb to 3m and hover for about 30 seconds. It will carry solar cells which charge up in the daylight. NASA officials are not hiding that this is a high-risk project. It is no surprise why. For comparison, in Earth's atmosphere, helicopters with turbine engines can fly as high as 7.5km. The maximum altitude of a helicopter in "hovering" mode is around 3.5km. As already mentioned, the Red Planet atmospheric conditions are similar to those on Earth at 28km altitude. Even taking into account the lower gravity on Mars, the helicopter blades should rotate more than ten times faster in order to lift the same mass. My trust in the ingenuity of NASA engineers is quite strong. However, from my point of view, helicopters are definitely losing to aircrafts with jet-propulsion engines as flying vehicles on the Red Planet.

Let's now descent from the sky down to Martian terrain. As you can imagine, there are no roads on Mars, and it is unlikely they'll appear in the near future. Driving on Mars could be similar to participating in the Dakar Rally, in its off-road special sections such as crossing dunes, rocks and ergs. We definitely need a true off-road vehicle for such challenging tasks.

We should also keep in mind another important would-be feature of our Martian vehicle: the availability of large internal space required for a life support system, storage of oxygen, food, water and consumables for a lengthy journey. Most importantly, we'll need fuel. We need something that looks like a large auto-caravan with off-road vehicle features like raised ground clearance and ruggedness and available four-by-four (or even six-by-six) drive.

We already discussed the lack of oxygen in Martian atmosphere and the necessity of carrying both oxidant and fuel on-board the vehicle. Here I am going to offer one conceptual solution which could kill not just two but a few birds with one stone. I am talking about hydrogen car technology, which has already been developed to an advanced level. The reaction between oxygen and hydrogen in a fuel cell supplies electricity to electrical motors exhausting pure water vapour into the atmosphere. The only significant difference is that water on Mars is quite a valuable commodity. Despite its relative abundance in Martian terrain mining, purifying and storing water may require significant resources and energy. A straightforward solution in these circumstances could be collecting exhausted water and storing it on-board vehicle for consequent splitting back into oxygen and hydrogen. If we're going to carry both fuel and water with us, why not store it on the roof of our vehicle? Let me remind you about radiation on the surface of Mars, comparable with the level of radiation in ISS. Most radiation arrives from the Martian sky above our heads due to the shielding effect of the planet's body. If we store liquid hydrogen, oxygen and water on the roof of the vehicle, we can use them as quite efficient shields against radiation. I've suggested storing oxygen and hydrogen as cryogenic liquids because the evaporation of oxygen provides significant cooling power which can be utilised for reducing more than ten times the infrared radiation heating of a hydrogen storage vessel. This thermal shielding could decrease hydrogen evaporation to the level comparable with fuel consumption rate.

The suggested approach has a few more benefits. The most important is that, during its operation, the fuel cell generates both electricity and heat which could be utilised for heating the cabin of our vehicle. Another benefit: we can make liquid oxygen storage a bit bigger than required for fuel purposes, therefore utilising that oxygen to help the crew breathe. Exhausted water also could be used for autonomous life support system.

A simple estimation of fuel consumption per 100km (assuming 100% efficiency) gives us around 40kg of oxygen and 10kg of hydrogen which results in exhausted 50kg (or litres) of water. Volume-wise, we have to add to a 50L water tank 35L of oxygen cryogenic storage and shocking 140L liquid hydrogen tank. Another reminder that it is impossible to trick nature: the density of liquid hydrogen is very low, which is one of the reasons why NASA is considering the usage of liquid methane instead of hydrogen as a propellant for rockets. In the case of surface transportation this is not a big problem; we can easily store all these liquids on the roof of our vehicle and improve the radiation shielding of the cabin. The problem we have to deal with in this case is that the centre of mass of the machine moves up, making the vehicle potentially unstable. The easiest solution for improving stability is increasing the base, or in other words, moving wheels away from the car's body. Once these features are implemented, our Mars transportation vehicle could look like a remote-controlled robot rover Lunokhod-1, only much larger.

THREE
CRYOVOLCANOES

In my early days in low temperature physics, I was completely consumed by exploring the fascinating world of cryogenics. Thanks to an almost limitless access to liquid nitrogen, I used to dip various objects and materials into the mysterious cryo-liquid and enjoyed watching the transformations that happened to frozen objects.

Those days, most postgraduate students in our Institute had two scientific advisers. The officially appointed adviser was usually a senior, well-established scientist; the second adviser – an informal mentor or a "micro-boss", as we used to call them – was a junior scientist, a few years older than the student. My "micro-boss" became a very good friend of mine. Let's nickname him Rebel. Initially Rebel favoured my explorer enthusiasm for playing with liquid nitrogen; after I poured liquid nitrogen on his precious possum fur hat that irreversibly affected the fur quality, he made a 180-degree turn. To even the score, he performed a very cruel prank, and then he offered me an olive branch in the form of an agreement that pranks are acceptable, as long as there is no harm or damage to personal belongings. After shaking hands to encourage my positive behaviour, he promised to show me the cryovolcano "Tyatya", as long as I withstood the agreement's trial period. This idea ignited my curiosity because the Russian word "tyatya" means "daddy" in English and the real volcano Tyatya, located in Kunashir Island, was well known for its volcanic hyperactivity.

Although I was intrigued, I didn't stop planning my response to Rebel's last prank. It wasn't easy keeping within the limits of our treaty, so it took me an unusually long time to prepare. After a few days of observation, I realised that every morning after sitting down at his desk, Rebel used to dump his heavy street shoes, changing into soft, light moccasins with a kauchuk sole, very popular in the Soviet Union in the eighties. The change turned the expression on his face into one of pleasure and comfort. After days of waiting, the time came to initiate my evil plan. In the morning, when Rebel approached our lab room, our roommate Valerij started a loud conversation in front of the door. This was my cue to act quickly. As soon as I heard the voices, I poured a small puddle of water under Rebel's desk, grabbed his moccasins and put them in a polystyrene foam box with a shallow pool of liquid nitrogen. It took just 20 seconds to cool the kauchuk sole (I'd tried a few times before to make sure I got the optimal time), after which I placed the moccasins in the shallow puddle of water exactly where Rebel had left them. As expected, the cooled kauchuk soles immediately froze the water underneath, gluing the moccasins to the floor. Once frozen, I walked out into the corridor, greeting Rebel casually, and quickly disappeared into the neighbouring room.

A couple of minutes later, Rebel broke into the room and gave me a sizzling look. Our roommate, also a participant in the prank, followed him. I tried my best to look as innocent as possible, pretending that I knew no reason for Rebel's furious gaze.

"Aha, you violated our convention!"

"What are you talking about?" I responded, trying to feign an innocent look of surprise.

"You glued my beloved moccasins to the floor with Stycast epoxy, inflicting damage to my property."

It is appropriate to note that polymerised Stycast epoxy is transparent and looks similar to ice. At that moment, Valerij broke into our conversation to ask for further explanation and details. Rebel began to explain the situation.

"I didn't do it," I said.

It was Rebel's turn for silence. One second, two seconds, three seconds. He asked for an explanation. I invited both colleagues to our lab room where I approached Rebel's desk, picked up his moccasins (the ice had melted by this point) and put them into the hands of a speechless Rebel. When Rebel reluctantly accepted that it was a nice prank and his property was not damaged, I was in seventh heaven. Finally, after a cup of morning tea he conciliatorily suggested that I was ready for the cryovolcano Tyatya demonstration and booked the performance for that same day, after lunchtime.

Before I get into the most important part of the cryovolcano story, I should describe the scenery around our laboratory. Just opposite our lab there was a small dark room used for processing photo film produced by an antediluvian analogue oscilloscope. This huge box was able to memorize a single pulsed signal for a couple of minutes with an option to capture it on photo film. To be honest, by that time, the oscilloscope had already been dysfunctional for many years; the dark room was used for working with photographic film to make prints and carry out other non-hazardous, chemistry-related tasks. An inalienable part of all photo rooms was a laboratory sink installed on the wall, shared with the male toilet next door. It should come as no surprise that the sink's waste pipe was connected to the same wastewater collector as the waste pipes of the urinals situated on the opposite side of the wall. Rebel had chosen the dark room's sink for the demonstration, his choice based on its large size and the tap's strong water flow. He also brought with him a storage dewar full of liquid nitrogen.

Rebel started the demonstration by opening the tap for a few seconds before closing it and generously pouring liquid nitrogen into the sink. Once in the pluming, the liquid nitrogen made a gurgling sound. Immediately after that, Rebel fully opened the tap… the Tyatya cryovolcano erupted! The sink ejected jets and clouds of the mist and spat droplets of liquid nitrogen in all directions. Clouds of mist quickly filled the dark room up to our knees, a picture that would ignite a heart attack for any Health & Safety Officer today. The eruption was accompanied by bursts of sound similar to those of a geyser. It was spectacular!

Our meditation was abruptly broken by our colleague, Nikolay, who leapt into the room with active gestures. Judging by his frantic manner, it was clear something even more extraordinary than the Tyatya eruption had happened.

He desperately gestured for us to follow him to the toilet. We stopped in the doorway as if frozen. A middle-aged gentleman was standing in front of a urinal holding both his hands on his private parts. He stared into the urinal intensely; the urinal was expelling wreaths of mist at his knees accompanied by an unpleasant gurgling sound.

"I haven't even started yet," he said in a low voice. Both Rebel and I choked with laughter.

Many years later, I learnt that the "cryovolcano" was not merely a figment of Rebel's imagination. Rather, cryovolcano is a completely credible scientific term which describes the kind of volcanoes that erupt water and other volatiles like methane, nitrogen or ammonia in the form of liquid cryo-lava, mist or vapour. During an eruption, a cryovolcano could form flows of cryo-magma, gas jets or plumes that look similar to the ones produced by usual volcanoes. That's where the similarity ends because the cryogenic environment changes the very nature of the eruption.

Cryovolcanoes are not common on our planet – apart from in cryogenic laboratories populated with over-enthusiastic students – though their close relatives, mud volcanoes and geysers, are quite numerous. Like cryovolcanoes, these eject water and gases, but at much higher temperatures (around water's boiling point or even higher), which makes them completely different. By the way, traces of mud volcanoes were recently observed on the surface of Mars.

Astonishingly, injuries caused by skin exposure to erupting substances may look quite similar, even though their nature is very different. In the case of a geyser, the exposure could lead to a thermal burn. In the case of a cryovolcano, exposure could result in frostbite. However, after an hour or so they will look very similar, like an ordinary blister. The bottom line is, please do not try making cryovolcanoes at home. Pain is almost unavoidable.

Although uncommon on planet Earth, cryovolcanism is common in other parts of our solar system. There are a few compelling pieces of evidence that prove its existence and even allow us to speculate on the possible mechanisms behind this wonderful natural phenomenon. With courage, I suggest that we already have enough knowledge to differentiate between the two types of cryovolcanism. The first relies on the existence of large volumes of liquid water underneath the cryovolcano; the second can happen in completely frozen, solid terrane.

To start with the first type: in our solar system, there are a number of celestial bodies including Europa, Enceladus, Ganymede and Titan where oceans of liquid water are thought to be present under a thick crust of ice. If you are interested in the astonishing paradox of how water can remain liquid in these deeply frozen, cryogenic worlds I invite you to read *Parallel Thought 3.1*.

In this type of cryovolcano, liquid water plays a role similar to the one magma does in our ordinary volcanoes. Same as magma, liquid water exists under the enormous pressure produced by the weight of a multi-kilometre thick icy crust. In the places where the ice layer gets thin, for whatever reason, water escapes from cracks in the crust, which can be opened and closed by tidal stresses. Coincidently, the places of escape demonstrate a significantly higher temperature than the surrounding area, which supports the suggestion of the close proximity of the crust surface to the large volume of liquid water, which is significantly warmer than the cryogenic environment of the crust surface.

These magnificent eruptions have been directly observed on Enceladus, the sixth-largest moon of Saturn, and Europa, the smallest of the four Galilean moons orbiting Jupiter.

The first sighting of a plume of icy particles above the Enceladus South Polar region came from images taken by the Cassini robotic spaceship in 2005. The scientific data collected during subsequent fly-bys of Enceladus allowed the creation of a detailed picture of the phenomenon. The cryovolcanic vents near Enceladus' South Pole shoot monstrous geyser-like jets of water vapour together with other volatile materials into space at supersonic speed. Some of the water vapour solidifies and falls back as snow – the cryogenic analogue of the volcanic ash – but the rest escapes into interplanetary space, feeding Saturn's E ring. Despite an initial impression of the plumes looking like discrete jets, later observations revealed that the plumes rather remind one of broad, curtain-like cloud which spans from the moon's surface to hundreds of kilometres into space.

The second direct observation of cryo-geysers occurred in 2012 when the Hubble Space Telescope acquired an image of Europa. The picture – surprise, surprise – turned out to be very similar to the Enceladus eruptions. The 200km high plume of water vapour with similar volatile materials was erupting from near its South Pole. The plume area also matches the location of a thermal hotspot on Europa's surface that was first detected by the Galileo spacecraft in 1999.

The indirect evidences of cryovolcanism have also been observed in the Sotra Facula region on Titan. The images of this area obtained by the Cassini spacecraft revealed three large conical features with material flowing outward, as well as several deep pits. According to the Cassini program scientists, all the information collected by the spacecraft pointed towards cryovolcanism.

Now I am inviting you to fast-forward our imagination to Enceladus' South Polar Region where this alien spectacle is happening in front of us. We are staying on an icy plane. It is the middle of a polar day and shiny white-blue terrain is in deep contrast with a pitch-black sky dotted with a myriad of bright shining stars. Somewhere behind us, the colossal Saturn with all its rings hangs in the sky. Tens of kilometres in front of us an enormous bright white wall rises from the icy plane to infinity in the sky. The wall doesn't look solid, but rather like an approaching dust storm in Sahara stretched upwards into the sky. What a magnificent view!

Occasionally we can spot vertical traces of ice particles falling at high speeds from the sky to the icy surface, like tiny meteorites. We catch a glimpse of them only on the pitch-black sky background. We also may be able to fill and hear these particles when they hit our helmet or shoulders of our space suit, like the first heavy drops of a spring rain.

By the way, a similar type of cryovolcano eruption should look very different on Titan. The reason for this difference is the very dense atmosphere of this moon in contrast to a near-vacuum on Enceladus or Europa. Actually, Titan's atmosphere makes the cryovolcano eruption image similar to one of an ordinary volcano here on Earth. On Titan a cryovolcano is expected to eject clouds of cryogenic ash – snowflakes, flows of cryolava – viscous salty water and to spit out cryovolcanic bombs, or lumps of ice. Similar but not quite the same: this picture lacks the most important feature of a volcanic eruption, the glowing magma and lake of fire in the volcano crater. No problem, we can easily fix this difference by putting on infrared radiation, IR vision goggles. This is the second time I am relying on this kind of visual aid; we first used it when we were chasing rainbows on Titan. Once the IR goggles are on, everything finally looks the same; cryolava and cryovolcanic bombs are glowing, as in our world. There is a reasonable explanation for this; electromagnetic waves radiated by all bodies at cryogenic temperatures have longer wave-length, so to adjust our vision to another wavelength range we need IR goggles. By the way, when seen through IR goggles a human without a spacesuit on Titan would also glow. To have the same glowing appearance in our world, in the visible part of the spectrum, this human-like creature should have a temperature around 500°C. Does this remind you of a character from Marvel Comics? The only problem with this is that a human without a spacesuit will not survive in Titan's freezing environment for longer than a fraction of a minute.

There is another infamous natural phenomenon which often follows major volcanic eruptions: the deadly pyroclastic surge. It was a pyroclastic surge caused by the eruption of Mount Vesuvius in 79 AD that completely destroyed the ancient Roman city of Pompeii and buried its inhabitants under a few meters of volcanic ash. In our world the pyroclastic surge is the gravity-driven clouds of a few hundred degrees' Celsius hot mixture of ash and gases which can travel with a speed of up to 500km/h. In Titan's world the pyroclastic surge could be similar gravity-driven clouds of a "cryogenically warm" mixture of snowflakes and gases which can travel at a few tens of km/h speed. Sounds like an ordinary snowstorm, doesn't it? As discussed in the Titan chapter, the only difference from a terrifying methane storm is that, at cryogenic temperatures, frozen water snowflakes are not sticky at all. Though a pyroclastic surge on Titan might look frightening, in reality it should be harmless.

An expected combination of conditions in cryovolcanic plumes on Titan could also be favourable for the realisation of volcanic lightning, which arises from static electricity generated by a collision of volcanic ash particles, or snowflakes in a cryovolcano's case. I hope this scenario offers a glimpse of hope to scientists that were so frustratingly fruitless in their hunt for lightning on Titan.

I've returned to Titan again as this is my favourite outer cryo world and I can talk about it for hours. Yet, I'm aware it is time to move onto the second type of cryovolcanism. This type happens on celestial bodies where large reservoirs of liquid water are entirely absent. Currently there is no clear understanding of the mechanisms behind these phenomena, though this does not stop us from discussing a few plausible ideas in *Parallel Thought 3.2*. Traces of this kind of cryovolcanism have been observed on the dwarf planet

Pluto, asteroid Ceres and moons Charon and Miranda. Mentioning Pluto is an ideal opportunity for me to confess that this largest known planetoid is actually number four on my list of favourite outer cryo worlds. The main cause behind my elevated interest is the remarkable visual similarity between Pluto's mountain views and snowy pics of the Swiss Alps. Regrettably, the Pluto-related information obtained by the New Horizons Mission and previous astronomical observations is not sufficient to fill a proper size chapter, but for me it is still enough to justify ***Parallel Thought 3.3***.

The most spectacular manifestation of the second type of cryovolcanism was captured by cameras of ESA's Rosetta spacecraft during its rendezvous with 67P comet discovered in 1969 by Soviet astronomers Klim Churyumov and Svetlana Gerasimenko and like all other comets named after its discoverers.

On March 12th 2015, Rosetta's on-board camera OSIRIS WAC directly observed, for the first time, a small outburst event starting from the initial phase through the evolution to its very end. Since the source of the jet was located on the not illuminated part of the comet's nucleus, it was assumed that the jet expanded into vacuum or at least into a very low-pressure gas. Though this bears a similarity to the cryo-geysers of Enceladus, there are two significant differences: their composition and scale. The Enceladus plumes contain water vapour with some volatile materials, while the comet 67P outburst jets consist mostly of dust particles mixed with volatile gases and some water ice crystals. The sizes of dust particles range from 1 micron to a maximum of 3cm. Another distinction is in the sheer scale of these spectacles. The hundreds of kilometres' high plume of the Enceladus-like eruption dwarfs any comet outburst (usually no more than a couple of kilometres high).

Later on, when many more outburst events were observed, scientists classified them into three different types. According to their morphological features the outbursts can be: broad fans, narrow jets and complex plumes. Rosetta has also discovered collapsed sinkholes of the order of a few tens of meters that were tentatively identified as outburst sources.

Now we have enough information to fuel another imaginary voyage, this time to the comet 67P. I invite you to close our eyes and let our imagination land on the surface of a cometary nucleus. Our first impression is that we are in the middle of a strange snowstorm. Strange because, despite the number of particles whirling wildly around us, we cannot feel the force of the blowing wind. That is because of the very low pressure of the gases which surround us. There is one important thing that we have to keep in mind when we are on the surface of a comet. The gravity here is extremely low. So, please avoid energetic flicks or jumps that can send you off into space at, or above, the comet's escape velocity, which for comet 67P is only around 3.6km/h. If, as a result of a reckless move, you are already moving away from the comet with a velocity higher than this, you would escape into space and disappear forever into the infinity of the universe – quite an unpleasant perspective, don't you think?

Suddenly, just a few hundred meters in front of us, a bright jet of dust and icy particles shoots off from one of the pits. A few moments later, we feel a light push accompanied by the quiet sound of a bursting party balloon. A whistling noise. We have been hit by the front of a faint shock wave generated in the first moment of outburst. We might also feel a light tremor from the ground. No matter how weak this disturbance, it could be strong enough to throw us out of balance because the extremely low gravity of the comet makes balancing our bodies vertically a very challenging task. If, thanks to our perfect body control, we managed to maintain equilibrium in an upright position, it is a good time to relax and appreciate the spectacle. The jet is bursting into space and its upper part fades away in a dusty haze of halo above our heads. The outburst noise is getting louder and slightly changing its tone due to increasing gas pressure around us, which nevertheless remains quite low. The whole outburst may take anywhere from several minutes to a few hours. Staring at this spectacle for longer than ten minutes would be tedious because the dynamics of the outburst barely change until the very last moment of the event.

An optimal choice of the observer's position is crucial for enjoying the spectacle of the cometary outburst to its full extent. If we are too far away from the outburst the view could be obstructed by the dust cloud, which usually wraps the cometary nucleus, but if we are too close, we can be smashed by the ejecting jet. The velocities of outburst plumes range from several tens to more than a thousand kilometres per hour. The first moment of the cometary outburst started right under our feet is similar to the explosion of an anti-tank mine, the only difference being that the remains of this unlucky observer would be launched into space with the speed of a jetliner. As we can see, it is quite a dangerous place to be; the longer we stay, the higher the chances that the next outburst will erupt beneath our feet, especially if the comet is at its highest levels of activity in the weeks around perihelion. So, after few minutes of enjoying the outburst wonder, it'd be a good idea to return to the real world.

As I already mentioned, there is a geomorphologic (what a tongue twister) resemblance in the traces of cryovolcanism observed on Pluto, Ceres, Charon and Miranda, to volcanism on Earth that might arise from a physical similarity between highly viscous cryogenic substances and the silicate based magma. All the celestial bodies mentioned above are far away from the Sun, which makes them very cold places with a surface temperature as low as 40K (-233°C). They are also relatively small objects and in such freezing conditions cannot sustain a warm nucleus on a planetary evolution time scale. As a result of that, the liquid water should not exist even on a short time scale of hours, yet trails of solidified cryolava flowing from volcano-like craters have been observed on all of them. If we suggest that volatile materials typical for cometary outbursts like nitrogen, methane, carbon dioxide, ammonia or argon may have been erupted on some icy satellites, without water they could not form stable solids that can exist on the surface of a celestial body for a geologically long time; therefore, water constitutes an essential part of cryogenic magma. One of the possible substitutes to cryo-magma could be mixtures of water and ammonia or perhaps water and ethanol. In both cases the freezing point of these substances moves below 180K (-93°C). At temperatures just above freezing, they should have high viscosity. Hence, it is quite possible that these mixtures could demonstrate lava-like behaviour in a cryogenic environment. The cryo-magma still needs to be warmed to above melting temperature, which happens anyway during the pre-eruption phase when pressure and temperature in a cryo-magma chamber increases to the critical value at which the eruption kicks off. Some ideas where the pre-eruption heating energy might come from are discussed in **Parallel Thought 4.2**. After the start of eruption, the cryo-magma starts to flow out from the cryovolcano's crater. As soon as magma touches freezing ground outside the crater, it begins to cool and eventually solidifies in a similar way as hot magma on Earth. That makes the bottom part of the picture of the eruption quite similar to what we would see during a conventional eruption on Earth. The upper part is expected to bear similarities with cryo-geysers of Enceladus or outbursts on comet 67P. The reason for that is the very thin, almost non-existent atmosphere on all celestial bodies that are currently the focus of our interest. The scale of the upper segment of eruption could be placed somewhere between colossal Enceladus cryo-geysers and modest cometary outbursts with cryo-jets shooting tens of kilometres into space.

If we take a night photo of an erupting volcano on Earth, draw a horizontal line through the crater rim, cut the photo out following this line and then attach a photo of a cometary outburst jet on top, we'd get an idea of how cryo-eruption on a planetoid or moon may look like. Although I'd better stop myself right now to avoid imposing on you a picture that might have no connection to reality whatsoever. The entire image of the last type of cryovolcanoes was based only on a few observations of cryo-volcanism traces. The rest was just a figment of my imagination, which sometimes guides me in a totally inaccurate direction. Anyway, I believe that taking into account the explosive development of space technology, it won't be long before one of our robotic spacecrafts or advanced space-telescopes will capture a real image or video of a cryovolcanic eruption on one of these extremely cold celestial bodies.

This is more or less all I know about cryovolcanism, but before I come to the end of the chapter I would like to return once more to the *colour* infrared goggles, as these have become an essential accessory of our imaginary journeys to outer cryo-worlds. The reason I am so enthusiastic about using these gadgets lies in the obvious dullness of outer cryo-world landscapes in visible light due to the lack of colour. If we looked at images of these places, we'd realise that in visible spectrum they look a bit too black-and-white or, in the case of Titan, brown-and-yellowish. However, a modern thermal imaging camera could add shades of blue, green, red and yellow to our palette, if we just shift the whole spectrum from visible to infrared range. For example, if we use an infrared camera to look at hot tea in a mug, we may see a glowing red or bright yellow liquid, depending on the temperature of the brew. It should be especially spectacular if you look at hot tea when you are on the surface of a frozen river or glacier; the tea might become the brightest spot on the whole image. When doing it, I recommend not looking at your friend's glowing face; it may look quite scary.

PARALLEL THOUGHT 3.1.
HOW CAN WATER REMAIN LIQUID IN DEEPLY FROZEN WORLDS?

Jupiter's moons, like Europa or Ganymede, are so far away from the Sun that they receive a very small percent of the amount of sunlight that Earth does. In the case of Saturn's moons, Titan or Enceladus, sunlight's energy is even smaller: no more than 1%. It is not surprising though that the average surface temperatures on these moons stay around or even below 100K (-173°C), which makes them deeply frozen cryogenic worlds. By what means then could the water under the thick crust of the surface ice remain liquid?

Today, the scientific community is considering three major sources of heat that could keep water in a liquid state: radioactive isotopes decay, tidal heating and heat-producing chemical reactions.

At the beginning of the formation of all celestial bodies a huge heating energy has been generated by the decay of radioactive isotopes which resulted in the consolidation of rocky materials such as silicates and iron at the moons' cores surrounded by shells of ice mixed with frozen volatile materials. Over time the heat from the radioactivity has decreased to the existing level, which alone is not enough to prevent the subsurface oceans from freezing.

Nevertheless, it did not take long for scientists to spot another, more powerful source of heat that could keep an ocean's water liquid. As is quite common in celestial mechanics, tidal heating occurs as a result of the dissipation of an object's rotational and orbital energy due to the internal friction in the crust or core of the moon. Some numerical simulations suggest that this source of heat could keep underground oceans warm for billions of years.

The recently discovered presence of volatile materials like ammonia, methane or carbon dioxide in Enceladus water plumes detected by Cassini instruments has suggested a possibility of exothermic chemical reactions in its underground ocean. However, the most optimistic estimations of energy released by these would-be reactions give a level of heating which is negligible in comparison with the two other sources discussed above.

PARALLEL THOUGHT 3.2.
DRIVING MECHANISMS OF CRYO-ERUPTIONS ON DEEPLY FROZEN CELESTIAL BODIES

Based on common sense I would suggest that any violent eruption which happens on a deeply frozen celestial body would require a huge energy release in a time comparable with the duration of the eruption itself. For example, an almost instant, explosive release of heat caused by impacts of small meteorites is too short to drive cryovolcano eruption for hours, let alone days. A more realistic scenario would be the slow accumulation of energy in one form or another followed by a self-accelerated energy release triggered spontaneously upon reaching certain conditions.

The best candidate for this kind of scenario would be the tidal heating already mentioned above. The parameters of Pluto, Charon and Miranda orbits indicate a strong possibility of enormous tidal forces which could generate enough energy to melt cryo-magma and trigger cryo-eruption. Another important characteristic of the tidal heating is that it could happen over a few days' timescale, allowing the gradual warming up of huge cryo-magma volume to the point of spontaneous triggering of the eruption.

The second candidate is actually my favourite, because I happen to know a few interesting details about this phenomenon. This is a kind of thermal explosion driven by the recombination of radicals produced by cosmic radiation in cryogenic materials such as solid methane or deep-frozen water ice. The history of this phenomenon's discovery is quite noteworthy.

In the 1980s, a group of researchers from Argonne National Laboratory led by American nuclear engineer Jack Carpenter developed a neutron cooling device based on solid methane. During initial tests the vessel full of solid methane at around 10K was exposed to a hot neutron flux. After 21 days of irradiation in a stable condition, the temperature of solid methane suddenly started to rise in an explosive manner. That resulted in the melting and partial evaporation of methane and burst of the system vessel. After thorough investigation, Carpenter came to the conclusion that exposure of solid methane to neutron radiation for a few days could lead to a build-up of defects produced by radiation in the solid methane matrix. When a critical number of defects has been achieved, the spontaneous self-accelerated recombination process might occur. In other words, the recombination of defects produced by radiation releases a vast amount of energy, which heats up the cryogenic substance and that in turn accelerates the recombination process even further.

During one of the conferences Carpenter coined the term "burp" effect, which later became popular in the neutron scattering community. In his *Nature* publication[2] he also suggested for the first time that similar effects may occur in other cryogenic materials and may be responsible for the jets observed from commentary nuclei.

Ten years later the group of researchers from the Joint Institute for Nuclear Research in Dubna conducted studies of the properties of cryogenic materials exposed to intense

---

2   John M. Carpenter "Thermally activated release of stored chemical energy in cryogenic media" *Nature* **330**, pages 358–360 (1987).

neutron radiation. They not only reproduced Carpenter's methane results but, more importantly, observed violent burp effect in the cryogenic water ice. This observation suggests that burping may have a place in many other cryogenic solids.

How would this phenomenon drive a cryovolcano eruption? Let's assume that somewhere below the surface of a deep-frozen moon there is a hollow filled with solid methane, or water mixture with volatile substances. Even that far below the crust's surface, the cryogenic solid is still exposed to cosmic radiation. The level of radiation could be significantly reduced by the layer of crust, but the exposure to radiation might continue for hundreds of thousands, if not millions of years. During this period an occasional cosmic radiation particle breaks a molecule of methane or water into chemically super active pieces or radicals. However, due to the very low temperature of surrounding matter these radicals do not recombine, but rather remain frozen into the bulk of cryogenic material for a very long time. When the number of accumulated radiation defects reaches a critical value the self-accelerated recombination reaction could either start spontaneously or be triggered by a temperature change or other disturbance capable of providing enough energy for kickstarting the recombination process. Once started, the self-accelerating heating reaches the melting temperature of the cryogenic magma. At that point the molten magma starts releasing volatile gases, which leads to an increased pressure in the caldera. Now it is simply a question of time… when the pressurised mixture of cryo-magma and gases finds its way to the surface of the moon, boom, the eruption begins!

Another potential source of energy which is worth

mentioning is the solar heating, but it could play a significant role only in case of comets because all other celestial bodies of interest receive too little of it for powering the cryovolcano eruption. The solar heating of the sunlit side of the comet's nucleoid surface may lead to sublimation of the volatiles and to the formation of dust jets. Outbursts also might be triggered by thermal stresses linked to a rapid change in temperature. Anyway, it is a common knowledge that all comets show higher levels of activity in the weeks around perihelion – the closest position to the sun – as a result of intense solar radiation that caused the gas and dust to stream into space at an ever-greater rate.

Among other suggested mechanisms we can find fluidization of a weakly bound mixture of ice and dust initiated by a phase change boundary between amorphous and crystalline ice, decomposition of gas-clathrate hydrates, heat-producing chemical reactions and even explosive substances produced by the exposure of volatiles to cosmic radiation.

Between you and I, I have a feeling that we may remain unaware of driving mechanisms which are waiting to be discovered.

PARALLEL THOUGHT 3.3
PLUTO

In my list of wonderful celestial bodies, Pluto takes honorary fourth place after Titan, Mars and 67P/Churyumov–Gerasimenko comet. This is not because this dwarf planet is not interesting or mysterious enough, but because all the information available presently is much less detailed by comparison with what we know about the top three.

The high-resolution images of Pluto's surface obtained during the flyby of NASA's interplanetary space probe, New Horizons, in July 2015 have revealed a wide variety of landscapes, from mountains made of water ice to smooth nitrogen ice plains. The temperature on Pluto during the space probe rendezvous with the dwarf planet was around 50K (-223 C°), a temperature which turns water ice into rock-solid material capable of supporting sharp, high mountain peaks (several kilometres high), separated by narrow valleys. The upper slopes of the highest peaks are covered with a bright material which supposedly consists of methane ice that occasionally precipitates onto peaks from Pluto's atmosphere. All these bits of information pooled together instigate in my mind an image of Pluto's mountains which resembles in shape, scale and appearance the Swiss Alps on a clear, cloudless night, but without vegetation and traces of human presence. Pluto's moon Charon rising above mountain ridges may complement the picture as a brownish version of our moon. The only significant difference would be the dark brown-to-red colour of the water ice rocks. Wait a moment! We know that here on Earth, water ice appears in a broad variety of colours, from bright white to shades of blue and green. Why does the same ice appear dark brown on Pluto? The reason for this is a layer of brownish organic particles that covers the water ice surface on Pluto. These brown-red-orange particles are created in thin atmosphere made up of nitrogen, methane and carbon monoxide under the space radiation, the same phenomenon which is responsible for the orange-brownish haze on Titan.

As soon as we mentioned Swiss Alps my imagination jumped to alpine skiing and snowboarding. At temperatures around 50K (-223 C°), methane snow properties are similar to the water snow at sub-zero temperatures, so there is no risk of our skis or snowboards getting stuck on the solid methane snow slope, as might happen on Titan. We only need to keep in mind that the gravity on Pluto is extremely low, about half the gravity of Titan, which itself is not high at all. This will result in a very slow acceleration after starting skiing. As a compensation we could enjoy ridiculous jumps and ski acrobatics in slow motion. Pluto's ski season does not last year round. Pluto's weather may change quite dramatically as Pluto orbits the sun. When the distance from Pluto to the sun is at a minimum, temperatures could get warm enough for the ices to sublimate directly into gases, creating a thicker atmosphere. The methane in Pluto's atmosphere is a greenhouse gas and could further accelerate heating of the dwarf planet's surface. According to some models the temperature could even exceed the melting point of nitrogen, creating a possibility of the existence of liquid nitrogen on Pluto. If these models are correct Pluto would join Earth and Titan as a celestial body with a solid-liquid-gas hydrologic cycle. On a peak of the hot season we may see streams of liquid nitrogen filling up puddles and lakes scattered here and there on the great nitrogen ice plains, some kind of cryogenic marshes. The atmospheric pressure could rise significantly, enough to allow transport and precipitation of methane that can refresh brightness of methane snow fields on Pluto's peaks. As Pluto moves away from the sun, the gases re-freeze and the planet's atmospheric pressure drops to its lowest level.

Another remarkable feature of Pluto's terrain I cannot leave without attention is the dunes formed by winds blowing from the centre of Sputnik Planitia in the direction of the surrounding mountains. A few hundred-meter-high dunes about a kilometre distance from one dune to another likely consist of methane particles a few hundred microns in size, making them quite similar to dunes on Titan.

This is probably all I can tell, for now, about the distant, dim and extremely cold world of Pluto.

FOUR
A FROZEN LIFE

In starting this chapter, I enter an area which is far from my expertise. I sense I am now in a high-risk zone of crossing the line between reasonable suggestion and ridiculous fantasy. However, the urge to discuss the subject of life in outer cryo worlds with you is so irresistible that I am consciously stepping onto thin ice with the little knowledge I have. As I do so, I would like to unreservedly apologise in advance for all the nonsense I am about to write.

My interest in cryobiology started when I was a junior cryogenic engineer. Then, driven by curiosity, I was tirelessly dipping different objects into liquid nitrogen. Most of these objects were of biological origin like fruit, flowers or insects. One of the observations I made was that biological objects lose their scent in a frozen state, a piece of knowledge that has been stuck in my mind ever since one particular event.

I hope you remember the "very cruel prank" carried out by my micro-boss Rebel in retaliation for damaging his possum fur hat. I think it is now time to reveal the details of this embarrassing story. After the fur hat incident, I was on high alert, expecting retaliation from Rebel. He behaved as if the incident was already forgotten, of course to put my vigilance to sleep. Once, whilst Rebel and I were carrying a liquid nitrogen transport dewar, we passed a woman, and I commented on smell of her perfume.

"So, you don't like it?" Rebel innocently asked.

I replied that I found the smell too sweet and vulgar. I did not realise then that I had just given him a perfect idea for revenge. He managed to find the brand of this very perfume and freeze it, turning the smelly liquid into a scentless icy lump, to be kept frozen until a suitable opportunity arose.

It is relevant to mention that when I joined the Lab I was given a brownish colour laboratory gown, a great colour choice for hiding stains inevitably caused by oily pumps, compressors and other equipment. All other scientists would usually wear bright white lab gowns. Eggheads from the theoretical department were allowed to be casually dressed. In order to emphasise my belonging to a gang of tough low temperature physicists, I used to wear my new brown lab gown at every opportunity, whether attending business or even social events in the Lab.

This particular time, just before I left to a meeting of the young scientist's society, Rebel inconspicuously dropped the frozen lump of perfume into a side pocket of my gown. About ten minutes later, when sitting in the conference room full of young scientists, I began to notice an unpleasant smell coming from my pocket. Little did I know at that point that the perfume was melting. The intensity of the smell was getting stronger and stronger. When the odour became almost unbearable, Rebel, who was sat in front of me, turned back, an evil smile dancing on his lips.

"Aha, you decided to wear women's perfume. How weird…"

I put my hands into my pockets and sensed a cold, wet spot in one of them, instantly realising that this was Rebel's brilliantly executed retaliation that I'd been anticipating. In that moment, I wished the ground would swallow me up.

It was after this event that we set up an agreement that prohibited any personal harm or damage to personal belongings, which led to the cryo-volcano demonstration, the result of which was my lifelong passion for the cryovolcanism.

I am actually not alone in my abnormal interest in what happens with living organisms at low temperatures. There is a popular belief that at low temperatures an organism's life could be "frozen" or put on-hold with a possible revival once that organism is thawed back to comfortable conditions. This preconception was exploited in science fiction books and movies and became an integral part of contemporary pop culture. Occasionally interest in this cultural phenomenon is reignited by anecdotal evidence, like the case of 26-year-old Justin Smith from Pennsylvania.

In 2016, on Justin's way back home from a local bar in Tresckow, where he'd been drinking with his friends, he blacked out and spent more than 12 hours lying unconscious in the snow in sub-zero temperatures. When Justin was found by his father the next morning, he was literally frozen solid: no pulse or blood pressure. It is not, therefore, surprising that when the paramedics arrived following the emergency call they believed Justin was dead. When he was brought to the emergency department of a local hospital the doctor, who decided not to give up on Justin, hooked him up to an extracorporeal membrane oxygenation machine which pumps and oxygenates a patient's blood, essentially doing the work of the heart and lungs. This procedure is usually used to save patients whose lungs and hearts are damaged by flus or heart attacks. As Justin's body began to warm up, his pulse and blood pressure returned to normal. Throughout the next few weeks, Justin made a complete recovery. As a consequence of this ordeal he lost all his toes and little fingers on both hands from frostbite, but luckily had no lasting neurological damage.

It is scientifically proven that lowering the temperature of living organisms reduces their metabolic rate or, in other words, slows down all their biological processes. In small mammals like hamsters or mice this slowing down could even lead to a hibernation state characterised by low body temperature and slow breathing and heartbeats. This state is usually observed during the winter season. Large animals like bears also go into a deep sleep during the winter months, known as torpor. Like in hibernation, during torpor the heart rate is extremely low, but the bear's body temperature remains relatively high, which substantially increases the metabolic rate.

Hibernation is an exciting topic on its own, not least because it suggests that life could possibly be put on-hold. Regrettably, temperature-wise, hibernation is far from the cryogenic range, which moves this topic outside the scope of this book. If, like me, you are interested in hibernation, I invite you to continue the conversation in ***Parallel Thought 4.1***.

Returning to cryogenic temperatures, we can start from the fundamental limitations that water ice formation applies to life on planet Earth. There are no living organisms in our biosphere which can fully function or reproduce at cryogenic temperatures. Even if some of the plants, microorganisms and animals could revive after spending months, or even years, in a frozen state, this condition proves lethal to mammals and other advanced forms of life. The formation of water ice crystals at sub-zero temperatures can damage living cells, which subsequently may lead to the death of an organism. In extracellular and intracellular spaces, the ice forms only from pure water and excludes any dissolved solutes into the residual aqueous volume. As a consequence, cells become extremely dehydrated which can lead to deadly consequences. Isn't it ironic that the very same water which gives us life kills us at sub-zero temperatures?

Modern biotechnology has found a way to mitigate some of the consequences of ice formation. The cryopreservation of cells, embryos, and even small samples of tissue is broadly used in medicine, agriculture, and in rare and endangered species preservation programs. I have to admit that I am fascinated by cryopreservation, but because it has nothing to do with outer cryo worlds, this topic once again falls outside the scope of the book. I invite you to continue this discussion in ***Parallel Thought 4.2***.

All living organisms which survive freezing below 0°C use different anti-freezing strategies to prevent ice crystal formation in their tissues.

Wood frogs, for example, found in Alaska and polar

regions of North America, have special proteins in their blood that cause the water in the blood to freeze first. Once nucleated, the ice sucks most of the water out of the frog's cells. Simultaneously the frog's liver produces glucose, which helps to keep the remaining water in the frog's cells and, at the same time, significantly reduces the temperature of ice nucleation, keeping the cell's inner space in a liquid state. Up to 70 percent of its body can be frozen, including the brain and the lens of its eye. As a result, the wood frog's heart completely stops, as do its muscles and breathing movements.

The arctic woolly bear caterpillar can survive the polar extremes of the Arctic zones of Canada and Greenland by accumulating sugars in its blood that work like antifreeze and protect the cells in sub-zero temperatures.

The Alaskan darkling beetle can withstand temperatures as low as -60°C (213 K). The beetle uses similar sugar-based antifreeze agents together with the aid of oily compounds that prevent ice formation in the beetle's cells. However, to my knowledge, no multicellular animal can survive being frozen to really cryogenic temperatures except the tardigrade.

The tardigrade is one of the world's toughest creatures known to science. This extraordinary resilience is partially responsible for tardigrades' extreme popularity in the media and on social networks. A likely larger portion of their fame is owed to their extreme cuteness. The first time I saw a tardigrade, I could not believe that I was looking at a product of natural evolution and not at an image invented by the Nintendo cartoonist responsible for Pokemon characters. While I'm on the subject, how about a new Pokemon, called Tardi, whose main power would be 100% protection from the attacking powers of all other Pokemon? This "invincibility" in combination with extreme cuteness could quickly make Tardi the most desirable Pokemon for collectors.

I am referring to the tardigrade's cuteness assuming that you have seen images of these animals before. In case you have not had the pleasure, let me sketch you a picture. Tardigrades are tiny animals about 0.5mm long when fully grown. They are also known as water bears because of their appearance and because their movement resembles a bear cub, but with four pairs of legs instead of two. Tardigrade legs usually have four to eight claws, which I imagine are very handy if you spend your life in mosses and feeding on plant cells, algae and small invertebrates.

The first time scientists realised that water bears can survive being frozen for a long time was when a group of Japanese researchers thawed Antarctic moss samples stored at -20°C for over 30 years. The thawed sample was loaded into water and soaked for a day. After that, individual tardigrades were retrieved and studied under the microscope. In a few days, the tardigrades returned to normal functioning and one of them even managed to reproduce. This remarkable result triggered a broad range of research where tardigrades were exposed to cryogenic temperatures, high levels of radiation, vacuum and other extreme conditions. Scientists have found that if tardigrades sense approaching hard times, the organism produces a mixture of proteins with other substances, which replaces water in their cells. In this state a tardigrade can survive in an extreme environment for years. Once the favourable external condition returns, water will refill the cells dissolving the cryo-protective mixture and the water bear will spring back to life.

The main conclusion of these studies was that tardigrades could survive even in outer space, which makes the water bear a superhero that could, in principle, exist even in a Martian environment. As we already discussed in the Chapter Two dedicated to Mars, the surface temperatures there may reach as high as 20°C. Some exotic places such as underground cavities or geothermal springs could lead to the presence of liquid water for a timescale long enough to support the life cycle of tardigrades. Of course, water bears would also need something like moss or algae to provide food and a habitat which, I'm afraid, stretches the idea slightly beyond the realms of the reasonable.

Realistically speaking, extreme conditions on Mars make the existence of any multicellular form of life very unlikely. That is not necessarily the case for microbes which are a lot more resilient and adaptable to harsh environments and could exists in places completely inhospitable to complex organisms.

In the world of planet Earth, the microbial life thrives on the bottom of the deepest Mariana trench, in waters of the Antarctic Lake Vostok buried under 4km of thick ice sheet, in super-dry sands of the Gobi desert and in a black smoker hydrothermal vent on the ocean floor in the middle of the Atlantic. The range of microbe's habitat temperatures spans from − 20°C for cold-tolerant bacteria that continue growth and metabolism at sub-zero temperatures, up to +60°C for extremophilic bacteria which live in hot springs in Yellowstone. The microbial life can survive high doses of radiation, high pressures, vacuum, dehydration and extremely toxic environments, deadly for other species. Certain bacteria have the ability to survive multiple freeze-thaw cycles which makes them even more relevant to the topic of this book. It is not surprising though, that scientists are specifically focusing on the possibility of microbial life in their epic search for life on Mars.

The area of possible habitat of the microbial life on Mars is already quite defined by the knowledge accumulated in the numerous Martian missions. The microscopic organisms cannot survive on the surface of Martian terrain due to strong ultraviolet radiation. They also may need at least a few meters' thick layer of Martian soil to protect them from particles shot into space during solar flares and galactic cosmic rays. This pushes possible evidence of life into the subsurface, away from present-day harsh surface conditions.

The most important precondition for the existence of all forms of microbial life is the presence of liquid water, which is required for the functioning and reproducing of organisms. That is why NASA has pursued a "follow the water" strategy on Mars. Actually, it may be not so difficult because of abundance of water on the planet. More than four billion years ago, when Mars was warmer and wetter it could have held enough water to cover its entire surface in a layer between 100m and one kilometre deep. About three billion years ago Mars begun the transition to much colder and dryer place. Small amount of water has escaped into space due to the weak magnetic shield of the planet, but most of it is still on the planet either in frozen state or trapped in minerals and buried in the planet's crust.

In recent years, NASA's approach received a huge boost. In 2018 researchers used data from the MARSIS radar onboard of ESA's Mars Express spacecraft to report signs of a 20km-wide subsurface lake located 1.5km under layers of ice and dust in Mars' South Polar Region. There might be not enough heat at these depths to keep the water in a liquid state, so scientists suggested that water could contain high concentrations of dissolved salts that could significantly lower water's freezing point. For example, water with dissolved salts of magnesium and calcium perchlorate can remain liquid at temperatures down to -123°C (150K). Some known species of microorganisms are adapted to life at high salt concentrations, but the range of conditions microorganisms can withstand is more limited when environments are both very saline and very cold: a double whammy effect.

There were other observations which may provide circumstantial evidence of life activity. Most puzzling of all is the rising and falling levels of methane and oxygen in Martian atmosphere. What is behind that is still a huge question. Both gases can be produced through organic processes by some life forms. Both can also be produced through geological processes.

In recent years NASA and European Space Agency, in collaboration with Roscosmos, have been planning astrobiology missions with goals to search for signs of past life on Mars. Each team is planning to lend their robotic rovers in sites that most likely have been habitable in Martian past. Both rovers have highly sensitive spectrometers which could identify faint bio-signatures. What's more, the ESA's Rosalind Franklin rover is equipped with a sub-surface core drill capable of collecting samples from two metres underground.

I can understand the modesty of space agencies in setting mission goals which are as broad and vague as "search for signs of past life." If you ask the government for billions of dollars, pounds or euros for a highly risky space mission, it is wise to set achievable goals. Indeed, even an absence of past life signatures on Mars would be a valuable scientific result, worth every penny.

In case of discovery of signatures of life, which ceased to exist a long time ago, the mission teams will bathe in glory and justify government spending on future missions for a long time to come. It is believed that, billions of years ago, Mars used to be a lot more hospitable to life with milder temperatures, higher density of atmosphere and an abundance of liquid water. If life began, it would evolve on Mars in unique ways that make it a highly desirable subject for astro-biology and astro-palaeontology research.

Finally, if life's presence were to be discovered on Mars, then it could change the paradigm of science completely. This discovery would quite possibly influence the direction in which human civilisation evolves.

Enough about microbes; their microscopic scale limits

my imagination. Have you ever dreamed about microbes? I have not. I find it much more interesting to think about objects comparable in size with us humans. Oddly enough, there are quite a few places in the Solar System which hypothetically could host complex life forms. One advantage is that, compared to Mars, little is known about these other places other than their possible existence. This opens almost boundless fields for thought; the less we know for certain, the wilder our dreams could be.

The most promising places for hosting complex life are extra-terrestrial oceans of liquid water thought to be present under the thick crust of ice on Europa, Ganymede, Enceladus or Titan. We already discussed the paradox of how water could remain liquid on frozen moons in **Parallel Thought 4.1**. To complete the picture, we need to mention the possibility of existence of smaller liquid water lakes hidden under the icy crust on Ceres, Pluto and even Mars but they are dwarfed by the vast oceans of Jovian Moons. Hidden under 10 to 30km thick outer crust, the Europa's ocean is expected to have slightly more than two times the volume of Earth's ocean and may be about 100km deep.

To set the scene for our journey, we first need to place the likenesses anchors in our minds. Let's start from similarities between oceans on Earth and on Europa.

Water pressure is the most important parameter which influences the diversity of marine life forms. The pressure is defined by depth, water density and gravity. Assuming that water density is similar in both oceans and the density of ice is not far from the liquid value, we can set up a comparable pressure scale. The gravity on Europa is about 7.5 times smaller than it is on Earth. That gives us a pressure just below Europa's ice crust between 130 to 400 times that of atmospheric pressure on Earth. For comparison, the pressure at the bottom of the 11km deep Mariana trench, the deepest on planet Earth, exceeds 1,000 atmospheres. On Europa it is the equivalent of 80km depth measured from the surface of the moon. That gives us a layer of liquid (50 to 70 km deep) under Europa's ice crust at pressures similar to Earth's oceans. The volume of this layer alone is comparable with the total volume of all the oceans on Earth.

The influence of gravity on the evolution of species poses an interesting question in itself, but completely falls out of the content of this book. If you are still interested in this subject, I invite you into *Parallel Thought 4.3.*

Returning to the main subject, what do we actually know about life in the deep waters of the Mariana Trench? First of all, there are the common inhabitants of the ocean floor: sea cucumbers, which play an important role in the marine ecosystem. Sea cucumbers help recycle nutrients by breaking down the organic matter produced by life activities of marine organisms. The sea cucumbers are, however, not lonely on the seabed. They are joined by large, single-celled organisms known as foraminifera, which are a bit like giant amoebas encapsulated into solid shells, reaching up to 10cm in diameter.

A few kilometres above the Mariana Trench seabed, the deep-sea explorers observed a giant shrimp-like animal amphipod and deep-water cephalopod: a relative of the octopus. In 2014 marine biologists found a big surprise waiting for them; a previously unknown species of snailfish was captured by a robotic camera, swimming at 8km below the surface. Scientists think that this might be the limit at which fish can survive, meaning that the absolute depths of the Trench probably can't support fish simply due to the constraints on the physiology of vertebrates. In terms of pressure/depth scale of the Europa moon, the habitable zone for this fish would be somewhere around 60km below the surface.

While Mariana Trench deep waters are capable of supporting the lives of some large organisms mentioned above, they are mostly dominated by the ubiquity of bacteria. It is not that surprising, given that in laboratory conditions some bacteria can survive pressure up to tens of thousands of atmospheres. With no light getting anywhere near the sea floor, the next question would be what these organisms eat. Bacteria are able to survive at these depths, feeding off methane and sulphur emitted from the crust. But many will rely on what is termed "marine snow": little bits of excrement or fragments of rotting matter that float down from the surface.

We already mentioned another obvious similarity for both the depths of the Mariana Trench and waters of Europa's ocean: an almost complete absence of visible light. So, how do organisms adapt to the darkness of deep waters? Some creatures, such as the dragonfish or certain species of jellyfish, produce their own light in order to attract prey, mates, or both. Others, which would prefer to be invisible, either become transparent or their skin acquires the ability to absorb any light that has managed to make its way down to the depths.

It does not seem like a crazy idea that organisms that live in complete darkness could develop alternative sensing mechanisms for navigation in the absence of heavenly sources of light such as the Sun, the Moon or bright stars. NASA Chief Scientist James Green hypothesised that if creatures were to be living in Europa's subsurface ocean, they may have a big eye, sensitive to infrared radiation irradiated by Jupiter and penetrating ice sheet. The positions of Jupiter and the Sun in the sky of tidally locked Europa could provide relatively simple and efficient means of navigation for such creatures.

By the way, the Mariana Trench is not the only place on Earth that resembles the alien oceans of Jovian Moons. There are also the dark and cold waters of the Arctic and Antarctic Oceans, particularly those parts that are covered by thick layers of ice. I think it is worth mentioning these places because of their peculiar environmental influence on marine animals.

Recently surveys of Antarctic marine life have found small mobile organisms at the surface of boulder that lies on the seafloor beneath 500 metres thick floating ice shelves. The boulder is a home to a stalked sponge, non-stalked sponges, and unidentifiable stalked creature that might be a kind of carnivorous demosponge. The organisms survived in total darkness and -2C° temperature. The food they ingest thought to be dead plankton from open waters carried by strong water currents for more than 1000 km before reaching them.

Over a century ago, members of the earliest expeditions to the poles recorded unusually large body sizes of familiar species. This phenomenon has become known as polar gigantism. The cases of polar gigantism have been reported among many species of marine organisms including, and not limited to, sea butterflies, octopuses, marine worms, crabs, lobsters, sponges, and starfishes. Scientists still have no clear explanation why it happens in such a strange way, apart from accepting that the combination of polar water conditions – such as coldness and darkness – is somehow behind the driving mechanism of polar gigantism.

I hope you would agree with me that we may already have enough details of life in deep, cold and dark waters of Earth's oceans to feed our imagination, but what do we actually know about the oceans of Jovian Moons apart from volume, depth and pressure?

The most valuable information so far is the chemical composition of the Enceladus cryo-geyser's vents obtained during Cassini fly-bys over Enceladus' South Pole. In the water plumes, Cassini instruments have discovered the presence of volatile materials like ammonia, methane or carbon dioxide but have also found traces of simple organic compounds and complex macromolecules. Furthermore, the high level of salinity and alkaline of Enceladus plume's water could be a consequence of the serpentinization of non-metallic rock. This reaction leads to the generation of hydrogen which could be used by microbes, if any exist in Enceladus' ocean, to obtain energy by combining the hydrogen with carbon dioxide dissolved in the water. This chemical reaction produces the methane detected in the water plumes and is present at the root of the tree of life on Earth.

The idea that the cradle of life on Earth was situated around deep sea hydrothermal vents has recently received a strong boost. In the journal *Nature Ecology & Evolution,* a group of scientists led by Professor Nick Lane from University College London have published the results of an experiment where they replicated the hot alkaline conditions typical of thermal vents. They showed that under these conditions the mixtures of single-chain amphiphiles, abundant in hydrothermal vents, form vesicles or protocells, regarded as a vital basic building block for life. They came to the conclusion that alkaline hydrothermal conditions not only permit protocell formation at the origin of life but actively favour it. Authors of the paper have also suggested that their results provide hope of finding life on other planets and moons where there are oceans and similar conditions.

If a primitive microbial life emerged in Enceladus' ocean billions of years ago, it is reasonable to suggest that during this astronomical period, in stable and relatively life-friendly conditions, the evolution might produce remarkably complex life forms. This might seem a long stretch of logic, but why not embrace the wildest of dreams?

Now that we have built enough "likenesses anchors", let's turn to the hypothetical International Europa Surface Station.

Immerse yourself in this: you're in a shuttle elevator, due to depart to the sub-crust compartment at any moment. Keep your seat belts fastened for the whole journey. The gravity on Europa is weak, and accelerating inertia may smash unfastened bodies into the lift's ceiling. It takes about half an hour to reach the ground level of a 25km deep elevator shaft. The elevator doors slide open and we enter the subsurface compartment, which consists of a surprisingly small service room and two airlock portals. The large one allows loading of the bathyscaphe into the service room for repair and maintenance and the smaller gate provides direct access into the cabin of docked vessels for the pilot and researchers. The small size of the service room is the consequence of an enormous differential pressure between outside ocean waters and the compartment interior; this applies tough requirements on the room's size and the wall's strength. That explains why the surface part of the station is many times larger, allowing space for numerous laboratories, workshops, apartments and even for an astro garden and swimming pool where we could enjoy swimming in a low gravity environment to its full extent.

Apart from the bathyscaphe, the sub-crust compartment hosts two deep-water robots-explorers. In a corner of the room, a few engineers are bowed over one of the robots held by a gigantic robotic hand, supposedly doing some maintenance work. All people in the room, including us, are dressed in special insulation suits in order to prevent biological contamination of the alien world outside the walls of the sub-crust compartment.

Before we are allowed into the shuttle elevator, all of us put on biological suits and undergo decontamination. In human absence and before robots could be offloaded back into the ocean, the space of the empty service room is illuminated by a high-power UV light for killing all living organisms to provide an extra level of protection for the indigenous world of the Europa Ocean.

After a quick chat with the engineers, preoccupied with the maintenance of the robotic vessel, our pilot opens the gate and invites us into bathyscaphe's cabin. Unlike ancient bathyscaphes our vessel does not have porthole windows. Instead almost the entire inner surface of the cabin is covered by 3D screens which display pictures captured by external video cameras. For us it is like sitting inside a cabin made of highly transparent glass. In front of the pilot seat, there are virtual windows with a dashboard and communication interfaces. An individual interface window could be opened anywhere on cabin surface by a light touch of a hand.

After adjusting seats, we listen to the safety instructions. Once formalities are over, the bathyscaphe undocks from the gate and starts descending into a darkness of the Europa ocean deep waters.

"There is not much to see until we reach the Bruegel Plato." The pilot informs us.

The IESS subsurface compartment stays about 20km north from the edge of the Bruegel Plato, which rises more than 30km above the seabed. The IESS location has been chosen for its close proximity to a group of gigantic hydrothermal vents in the middle of the plateau. These wonders of nature attract enormous interest from geo- and planetary- scientists, but most importantly they are sources of the essential elements required for a variety of life forms to flourish above the Bruegel Plateau. Plumes ejected from the vents are rich in hydrogen, methane, ammonia and other chemical compositions, which provide food and building blocks for microorganisms that support a variety of life forms, quite different from those we know.

The mission of our expedition is to replace tracking buoys attached to the gigantic snailfish that is, in fact, a completely different organism from both biological and physiological points of view, named snailfish only because of the resemblance in shape and the way it moves. These illusive creatures are hovering through upper layers of hydrothermal vents plumes rich in euro-plankton (microorganisms of different kinds that provide food for larger animals like snailfish). The tracking buoys installed on the animal need their batteries replaced.

To pass the time our pilot shows us a video captured during the last visit of a deep-water robot to Bruegel Plato. After opening a virtual screen, she activates a 3D video record. As the video plays, she comments on the most interesting observations. She is a good storyteller, quickly grabbing all of our attention.

The video starts from the pitch-blackness of Europa's ocean-deep waters. Suddenly a ray of light snatches out of darkness the edge of the Bruegel Plateau. The dark grey rock of the cliff is disappearing into the ocean abyss. A strange forest of alien forms of sea-vegetation covers the top of the plateau and spans as far as the robot's light source allows us to see. When the robot gets closer, we start to see the details of these bizarre ocean plants. They resemble gigantic chanterelle mushrooms with large round caps. A few spread out roots tightly hold the plant's trunk. The plant body has a dark brown colour, contrasted with the light grey shade of the ground soil. Upon closer examination, we realise that mushroom-like plants are slowly swinging. The movement starts from the plants at the cliff edge, probably driven by convection flows, and propagates in a wave-like manner into the depth of the forest. The ground between the plants is covered with white spherical and egg-shaped formations. Their perfect forms and complex surface patterns suggest life-related origin.

Closer to the forest, the robot's lighting control starts reducing the brightness and increasing the areal coverage. My colleague glimpses glowing neon-blue stripes wriggling in the darkness between the trunks and roots of the mystical forest.

"What is that?" He asks, pointing at the flared-up trace.

The question puts a smile on the pilot's face. After a short pause, she responds, "Well spotted! You touched on the most exciting subject I could possibly talk about, so please prepare yourself for an endlessly long and passionate talk."

The emotionless voice of the bathyscaph's AI system interrupts her with an info-message, "The vessel is approaching a flock of jelly-blobs."

"Okay, we should have enough time to talk about that on the way back. For now, look outside."

The pilot ends the video and dims a light in the cabin. We realise that the water around us is not as transparent as it was at the beginning of our journey, likely a consequence of the euro-plankton. Despite the relative muddiness of the water, we can still see that we are surrounded by a surrealistic cloud of transparent knödels. These basketball size objects, called jelly-blobs according to our pilot, contain an internal structure that *shines with all the colours of the rainbow. The pattern of the structure is changing slowly.*

As the pilot explains, these creatures feed on euro-plankton, which they filter out when pushing surrounding water through their internal organs. Researchers do not know yet in detail how they function and reproduce, but have a few working hypotheses. One of these is that the glowing plays an important role in defence and reproduction. It is also accepted that dead organisms do not glow. To demonstrate that, our pilot switches on a holographic sonar and we immediately recognise a few more blobs, which were almost undistinguishable in the visible light. Surprisingly almost all dead jelly-blobs are covered with inch-long black creatures resembling shrimps or tardigrades. Their front legs are constantly moving, cutting out small pieces of the blob's flesh with tiny claws and delivering them into their mouth holes.

"Vulture shrimps," the pilot says. "They only attack jelly-blobs if they are not glowing, which means that they can probably detect a visible light. Fully functioning jelly-blobs have thousands of tiny, highly poisonous stings imbedded in their skin, so if anything touches them, they simultaneously unleash a few spring-loaded stings in the direction of the touch. One is enough to kill a vulture shrimp. Products of vulture shrimps' digestion and the remains of jelly-blobs slowly precipitate to Bruegel Plato and feed the forest of look-like-mushrooms trees."

It is about half an hour after we leave the flock of jelly-blobs when bathyscaphe's AI informs us that we are approaching the target of our mission: snailfish with installed tracking buoys. The pilot abruptly stops entertaining and focuses on control monitors. A holographic sonar image of the snailfish appears on the display and leaves us utterly speechless. Its inferior mouth creates a sad facial expression. Few pairs of whiskers that look like small antennas add more creepiness to the image of this creature, which is a few meters long and with an eel-like tail. The snailfish does not have eyes in the literal sense of the word, but a black semi-spherical swell on top of its head resembles an eye of Cyclopes, a character from Greco-Roman mythology. As we learned, this infrared-sensitive organ facilitates the navigation of the snailfish in the dark waters of Europa Moon Ocean.

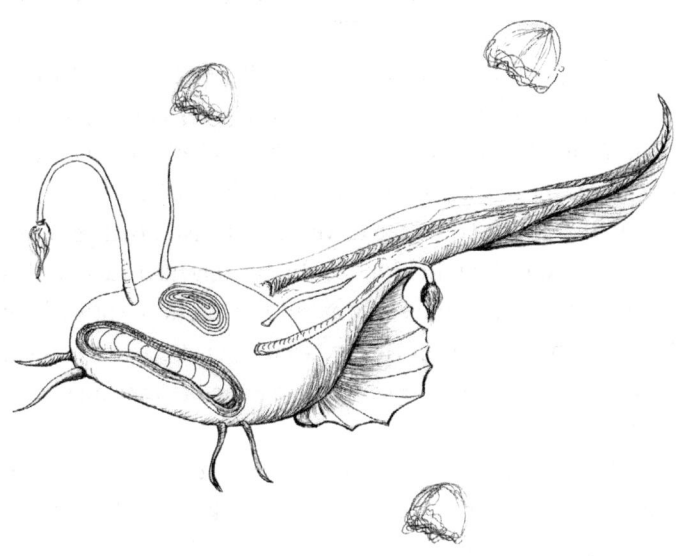

After the bathyscaphe's AI informs us that the snailfish is within reach of the submersible robots, the pilot activates the buoy replacement procedure. Two robots undock from external pylons and head to the target of our mission. In close proximity to the animal, one of the robots places itself under and another above the snailfish. Then they synchronously

approach the body and install two tracking buoys by pumping liquid from suction cups, which maintains connection to the skin. Immediately after that, old buoys detach themselves from the snailfish and are collected by robots. The tracking buoy contains a number of smart sensors that measure and transfer values of temperature, pressure and a few other parameters of the body and surrounding environment. It also provides information about location of the animal. A quarter of an hour later submersible robots dock on pylons and bathyscaphe's AI congratulates us all with the successful accomplishment of our mission.

After giving a quick instruction to the AI to return back to the base, our pilot turns to us and with undisguised pleasure says, "Now let me tell you about the Grand Centipede of Europa Moon, the most fascinating creature in the world!"

At this point I'd better leave the futuristic bathyscaphe, otherwise our imagination could be hijacked again, this time by the captivating story about the Grand Centipede of Europa. This would inevitably delay transition to our next topic: the utterly alien form of cryogenic life that may exist on Titan.

I left this subject until the end of the chapter because it represents another extreme. So little is known about these would-be-extra-terrestrial life forms that almost anything is plausible. As I mentioned earlier in the Chapter 1 dedicated to Titan, we know almost nothing apart from that there is a glimpse of possibility of its existence.

Historically, it was believed that ribonucleic acids (RNA) were precursors to terrestrial life. However, recent research has shown that synthesizing RNA as well as other prebiotic reactions would require a higher concentration of reactants than what is seen in waters of ancient seas or lakes. This condition has been realised through the enclosure of a small volume of solution into a vesicle made from self-assembled lipid membrane. This also defined individual cells as separate from each other, creating the potential for competition and natural selection. It is an established fact today that all terrestrial cell membranes are composed of a bilayer of phospholipids.

The role of self-assembled membranes in evolutionary biology on Earth raises the question of whether non-aqueous environments can support any similar structure. Liquid methane is of particular interest, because it is the only liquid, other than water, that forms large reservoirs on the surfaces of celestial bodies. As you probably already guessed, I mean methane lakes on Titan. Whether the largest moon of Saturn can support any form of cell membrane is not certain. However, it is known that its surface hosts an undetermined process that consumes acetylene, ammonia and other volatiles that continuously precipitate from the atmosphere but do not accumulate. An assumption that this process could be based on any alien life form would require a phospholipid membrane analogue capable of functioning in liquid methane at cryogenic temperatures.

It may sound like a crazy idea, but recently a team of biochemists and astrobiologists from Cornell University have suggested that tar-like substances called tholins might form vesicles made from self-assembled "azotosome" membranes. Their computer simulations have shown that some candidates from this family of chemical compositions could self-assemble into membranes in liquid methane with mechanical properties very similar to properties of phospholipid membranes at room temperatures. Obviously, this is just the first step, but it opens the possibility of existence of oxygen-free cells that metabolize, reproduce and do everything in a liquid methane environment, that these cells would do on Earth.

A couple of years later, this idea received strong support. Using the Atacama Large Millimetre Array, or ALMA, observatory in Chile, astronomers have measured a large amount of vinyl cyanide, one of the candidates identified by Cornell's team, enough to form tens of millions of cell membranes per cubic centimetre in Titan's sea, Ligeia Mare.

I know that it is still early days, but this observation gives us a legitimate excuse to fantasise about would-be forms of life that may exist in Titan's lakes. Another important fact is that, at cryogenic temperatures, all chemical reactions happen at a much slower rate, which should significantly slow down the pace of evolution of what would be Titan's life. In a timescale comparable with the presence of life on Earth, the evolution on Titan would only result in relatively primitive forms of life: something like a gooey mould on pebbles in shallow waters of a lakeshore, or a floating colony of single cell organisms that resemble a drifting island of sea foam. Even if we switch our imagination into turbo-boost mode, the most complex organism I can get is a jellyfish-like creature, similar to the jelly blob we met on Europa, which glows in the dark to attract representatives of the opposite sex (or multiple sexes?) of the same species. I would also equip this creature with a deadly high voltage weapon, because accumulating charge is much easier in the cryogenic environment of liquid methane. This ability could be very handy as a deterrent to predators, if any would exist on Titan, or for keeping away unwelcome alien intruders from the distant planet Earth. There is no doubt that the presence of such a creature would make swimming in one of Titan's lakes a more thrilling experience.

The higher the possible similarity between the life known to us and an imaginary organism, the easier it is to come up with the possible image and simulate its behaviour in our mind. But, when talking about something which could not possibly have a resemblance to our world, describing it might require the superpowers of an intellectual giant like Stanislaw Lem. In his philosophical science fiction novel Solaris, Lem created an ocean planet which is sentient. Solaris' ocean complexity and its intellectual superiority is far beyond human comprehension. However, its natural curiosity causes it to send a physical human "simulacrum" to investigate human behaviour in close proximity. This remarkable sci-fi story gives me hope that most alien life forms could recognise each other even if they cannot comprehend each other's existence. Whether it is a colony of microorganisms floating in clouds of sulphuric acid in Venus' atmosphere, live minerals, or intelligent plasma puffs, we will still be capable of recognising them as life forms as long as we keep our minds open.

That's why scientists and philosophers are already working on a broader definition of life, incorporating life on Earth "as we know it" as well as the possibility of "life not as we know it" elsewhere in the Universe. Finding a comprehensive definition is expected to be a long endeavour, although NASA astrobiologists have already come out with a working version of life as "a self-sustaining chemical system capable of Darwinian evolution."

As we are quickly approaching the end of the chapter, it feels like a good time for a short summary. So far, there is no sign of complex life existence apart from on our precious planet Earth. However, in light of what we know, we cannot completely discard the idea of the existence of complex, maybe even intelligent, life not only somewhere in the distant Universe, but also in the system of the star called Sun.

PARALLEL THOUGHT 4.1
HIBERNATION

Hibernation is one of a variety of ways that lives react to decreasing temperatures in the environment. All of these ways have a common feature. Almost all living organisms in polar zones of our planet demonstrate a slowing down, or even a complete suspension, of their metabolism during dark and freezing polar nights. In the case of mammals, the organism's reaction to seasonal temperature drop is determined by the size, and consequently by the mass, of the animal.

Let's compare two extremes: a hamster and a bear. Despite remarkable difference in weight (a hamster is around 20 – 30 grams and a bear between 60kg and 600kg), their normal body temperatures are more or less similar: somewhere between 37°C and 39°C. In the hibernation state, a hamster's temperature drops to 4°C – 6°C and the metabolism rate (consumption of oxygen) decreases about 10 times. The heart rate of these little fluffy cuties drops a staggering 30 times. A bear's temperature in torpor decreases only by six degrees and its metabolism is half than in normal conditions. A bear's heart rate is also half of normal.

The main difference between hibernation and torpor lies in the way animals wake up. Unlike hamsters, bears can wake easily in case of alarm. Pregnant female bears can also wake up from torpor to give birth, then go back to sleep afterwards. Evolutionally, all bears' body functions during torpor are optimised to save as much energy and as many calories as possible. They are even able to turn their pee into protein through a clever urea recycling process. Despite all of these tricks, different functions of a bear's body work at different rates at low temperature; these functions are not synchronised as in normal conditions. This disbalance accumulates with time and, unlike a hamster, a bear needs to occasionally wake up to allow its functions to catch up.

For all hibernating animals the main condition for survival is to store as much energy as necessary for supporting the life functions during hibernation period, plus the calories required to restart normal functioning of the organism once hibernation season is finished.

How about the hibernation of us humans? Strangely enough there is not much information available in the public domain about the reaction of a human body when exposed to low temperatures. It might be explained by a secrecy that surrounds some organisations, which are naturally interested in the outcomes of this research. I personally have no doubt that there is great potential in applying this knowledge to practical medicine, particularly in the area of long space travel. Despite the scarcity of information, it is recognised that the temperature of the human body could be reduced to 25°C without serious health consequences. Below this temperature humans face heart failure, arrhythmia and cardiac arrest. We can conclude that humans have built-in mechanisms that prevent the organism from further cooling. Let me give a couple more anecdotal examples which illustrate the situation quite explicitly.

Audrey Mash was hiking in the Catalan Pyrenees in freezing weather on November 3rd, 2019. She experienced a six-hour cardiac arrest after developing hypothermia when the temperature of her body dropped to 18°C. Luckily for her and thanks to her husband, she was quickly rescued and taken by helicopter to a hospital in Barcelona. There, she was connected to an extracorporeal membrane oxygenation machine, the same procedure that saved Justin Smith's life. When Mash's body temperature had risen to 30°C, doctors revived her using a defibrillator. After spending six days in the intensive care unit, Mash almost completely recovered with no sign of lasting neurological damage.

In contrast to the previous case, the heart of Jean Hilliard from Minnesota did not stop. In 1980 Jean was on her way back home when her car skidded off the road and got stuck in snow. It was a cold winter night, the temperature around -30°C. Jean was wearing a coat, warm gloves and cowboy boots. After she realised that there was no way for her car to escape from the snow trap, Jean decided to walk to a nearby friend's house. She collapsed just a few meters from his door as hypothermia took hold. When Jean was found the following morning, she was frozen solid but still breathing. According to *The New York Times,* when she finally arrived at a local hospital her heart rate was just 12 beats per minute and her body temperature was 28°C. The medical staff thawed Hilliard with an electric blanket, and over the next several hours she made a full recovery.

The astonishingly lower temperature of Jean's body and the drop in heart rate (much more significant than for a bear in torpor) suggest that her metabolism might have been reduced more than two-fold; decreased human body temperature slows metabolic activity about five to seven per cent for every degree dropped.

Recently the idea of human hibernation received a significant boost. Analysis of fossilised bones of early humans excavated in a cave Sima de los Huesos in northern Spain lead palaeontologists to hypothesise that thousands years ago our predecessors might have been dealing with extreme frigid conditions by sleeping through the winter. Similarity between the pattern of seasonal lesions found in the human bones and lesions found in bones of cave bears suggests that ancient humans have experienced some kind of torpor state.

Although it is still too early for drawing conclusions from this discovery, it provides an extra foundation to the fantasists like myself that the hibernation-like state of human body could be used in long time space travel missions. As we already discussed in **Parallel Thought 2.1: Travel to Mars,** there are a few serious hazards that can turn long space travel into a risky venture. However, the use of human hibernation could significantly mitigate and possibly eliminate some major risks. Allow me to explain.

Let's start with the deadliest of all: space radiation. A simple trigonometric estimation gives us a possibility of squeezing five average sized people into a cylinder ~ 1.5m diameter and ~ 2m long. Of course, this tight packing gives astronauts little freedom to move, but they need little freedom in the hibernation state anyway. In the weightlessness of outer space there is no sense of up and down, so all positions in the hibernation module are equally uncomfortable. The reason I am so enthusiastic about squeezing astronauts into such a claustrophobic environment is because it offers an opportunity to make a highly efficient cosmic radiation shield around the hibernation module based on a superconducting magnet. The trick is that the smaller bore of the magnet allows for a higher magnetic field which more efficiently deflects particles of the cosmic radiation. Reducing the size of the hibernation module itself reduces the exposure to radiation and, last but not least, there are indications that mammals have a higher resistance to the radiation exposure and infectious diseases in a hibernation state.

The second serious hazard is a collection of sociopsychological problems inevitably emerging when a group of people are spending a long time in the restricted space of a spaceship. Here the advantages of hibernation are quite obvious; one cannot communicate or socialise and consequently upset or offend teammates when in the hibernation state. All these activities and their consequences are postponed until the return to active life.

The third benefit of hibernation is logistical in nature. Due to a significantly reduced metabolism in a hibernation state, the human organism should consume much less oxygen, water and nutrients. As a consequence, the human body would produce less faeces. Of course, the situation with humans is not as desperate as it is with bears; humans have no need to turn their pee into protein, as they have plenty of protein from their life support system. A slower metabolism could significantly reduce the weight of consumable stock, which in turn would expand the opportunities involved in a mission.

There is another advantage which could become important – or even vital – in a distant future: space flights could continue for tens, if not hundreds, of years. Perhaps hibernation is the most realistic way to expand human life to a duration which would make it possible to undertake long space missions.

It seems to me that we have collected more than enough hibernation related material to satisfy our imagination for the short imaginary journey to Mars. I say short, as most of the journey will be spent in an unconscious state. I do not know if humans can see dreams during hibernation; even if they could, these memories would be wiped out upon waking up.

Here we go. We slid into the hibernation capsule a few minutes ago, attached to a sliding couch and connected to a number of plastic tubes and electrodes. Though we are in a very narrow space, we are not uncomfortable, thanks to the cocktail of drugs entering our bloodstream. We can hear quiet, smooth classical music. The soft light begins to fade. Our eyelids get heavier and heavier until they eventually close. We are losing our thoughts... When we next open our eyes, we find ourselves in a softly lit capsule. It takes a few minutes for us to return to reality and recognise the space and situation we are in. We can hear pleasant music, more dynamic now. A few minutes later, the couch slides out of the capsule and we see happy faces – our teammates – and the reddish surface of Mars through the spaceship porthole. What a strange feeling, to close our eyes whilst orbiting our home planet and opening them when approaching Mars.

PARALLEL THOUGHT 4.2
CRYOPRESERVATION

Under low-temperature conditions (below 173 K), many plant and animal cells can be preserved successfully for years. This process is known as cryopreservation. In the last half a century, cryopreservation has made impressive progress from bio-medical labs into multi-billion-dollar business. From my point of view, it would be more appropriate to measure cryopreservation's success by counting the 8 million lives given to babies since the start of IVF treatment, which strongly relies on cryopreservation technology.

IVF, or In Vitro Fertilisation, is one of several techniques available to help people with fertility problems successfully conceive. During IVF an egg is removed from the woman's ovaries and fertilised with sperm in a laboratory. For a variety of reasons, eggs, sperm cells and embryos quite often need to be cryopreserved for a long time before they can be used in the final stage of IVF. In the last 15 years, the contribution of cryopreserved embryos to overall IVF pregnancy is close to 30%. In the most extreme case, a baby has been born from an embryo frozen for nearly 25 years, possibly the longest ever gap between conception and birth. Cryopreservation also facilitates many other technologies that play important roles in medicine, agriculture and the preservation of endangered species.

Currently, the main limitation of the method is the size of the cryo-preserved sample. Modern technology provides efficient preservation of small objects such as sperm cells or multicellular embryos under cryogenic conditions for many years. However, for biological objects of larger volumes, cryopreservation often fails because of damage caused by the formation of intra and extra-cellular ice crystals during cooling and subsequent heating.

The actual process of cryopreservation involves water extraction from the cell through extracellular ice formation. This requires the use of protective compounds such as certain sugars and proteins to safeguard membranes and enzymes against damage during dehydration.

In some cases, this problem can be solved through vitrification, a cooling method that leads to the solidification of water without the formation of ice crystals. However, the viability of this method is also limited by the degree of cryo-damage caused by intra- and extracellular ice crystal formation, as well as the toxic effect of high concentrations of cryo-protectants and osmotic stresses.

Cryopreservation of larger structures such as whole organs has remained beyond reach. This is due to problems with the homogeneous distribution of cryo-protectant agents and control of uniform cooling or warming. I should mention the remarkable success achieved in the cryopreservation of ovarian tissue skin grafts. The size of the tissue samples is about $1cm^2$ by 1.5mm in thickness, which is more than two orders of magnitude larger than the volume of a cryopreserved embryo.

Chemotherapy and radiotherapy have improved survival rates of patients with cancer. However, these methods can cause ovarian failure and infertility in women of reproductive age. Ovarian tissue cryopreservation and transplantation is not only important, but sometimes the only option for fertility preservation in patients with cancer who need immediate chemotherapy or do not want to undergo ovarian stimulation. In 1997, there were approximately one hundred live births as a result of the clinical application of ovarian tissue cryopreservation and transplantation. Encouraged by this success, scientists are now working hard on cryopreservation of other "large" organs like secretion glands, parts of blood vessels or the natural lens of an eye.

If you would like to learn more about cryopreservation, I would recommend one of my favourite books, *Life in the Frozen State*, edited by Barry J. Fuller, Nick Lane and Erica E. Benson[3]. The main conclusion of this enjoyable read is that our understanding of the biological and biophysical impacts of transit to and recovery from deep cryogenic storage are as yet only partial.

I cannot complete this Parallel Thought without addressing an elephant in the room: cryonics. Cryonics is the process of preserving a whole body in the hope that resuscitation and a cure are possible in the distant future. As of 2016, there were four facilities in the world to retain hundreds of cryopreserved bodies and more than a thousand people have signed up to have their remains preserved. All "preserved" bodies in cryonic storages were frozen following the then-established protocol which, as we know, does not work for large biological objects. Technically, this means "patients" are already dead and the probability of their reanimation is almost non-existent. This non-zero probability gives a hope which allows grieving family and friends to think about their loved one as if he or she is still alive, only frozen for an unknown time. From this point of

---

3   Barry J. Fuller, Nick Lane, Erica E. Benson, *Life in the Frozen State* CRC Press (2004)

view, cryonics might be perceived as a viable psychological remedy for dealing with grief and loss.

PARALLEL THOUGHT 4.3
INFLUENCE OF GRAVITY ON EVOLUTION OF SPECIES

Gravity is one of the fundamental parameters that has shaped the evolution of life. In contrast to temperature, composition of atmosphere or presence of water, gravity has remained unchanged since life sparked on Earth. In addition, the value of gravity is more or less the same everywhere on the surface of the planet. The constant nature of gravity made studying its effect on biological objects a very difficult task, until humankind managed to break into outer space. This breakthrough opened new opportunities for experimental biology and medicine and allowed biomedical research into almost zero gravity. Nevertheless, from an evolutionary point of view, all experiments in space have been conducted within a very short timescale. The fundamental question "What is the influence of gravity on evolution of life?" remains pretty much unanswered.

In the years 2015 and 2016, NASA scientists conducted a thought-provoking experiment hoping to reveal new information about the effects of microgravity on the human body. Astronaut Scott Kelly spent more than 340 days aboard the International Space Station. Meanwhile, back on Earth, his identical twin brother Mark was closely monitored by researchers; he served as a genetically identical ground control. Though Scott's overall health remained in good condition while he was on the ISS, several small changes were detected in comparison to his brother. During Scott's mission, his telomeres (the protective caps at the ends of chromosomes) became elongated, although the exact effect of this elongation remains unclear. Researchers also found abnormalities in several of Scott's chromosomes and some minor damage to his DNA, as well as changes in his gene expression. Scott developed thickening in his retina and in his carotid artery. There were also shifts in Scott's gut microbiome that differed from those of his Earth-bound twin.

The weakest point of the study is its extremely small sample size: one set of identical twin brothers. In such circumstances, it is not clear whether the changes in Scott's health are specific to his particular physiology or generally representative of most people under similar conditions. The main cause of these changes is also unclear. Would it be due to the influence of microgravity, radiation, psychological stress or habitable room limitations?

The very constant nature of gravity on Earth did not deter great minds from trying to understand its influence on living organisms. Around 400 years ago, this problem was first formulated and approached by the father of modern science, Galileo Galilei. His final book, *Discourses and Mathematical Demonstrations Relating to Two New Sciences,* contains a discussion of why it would be impossible to scale up an animal, tree or building to infinity. His approach was based on the idea that assuming a fixed shape for an object means its volume will increase at a much faster rate than its area. In practical terms, this means that, as an animal grows in size, its weight increases faster than the strength of its limbs and the rigidity of its skeleton. At some point, the animal collapses under the force of its own weight. It is for that reason that there could never be a Godzilla or King Kong on planet Earth.

Today, the scaling effect of gravity is well known to biologists. The mass fraction of body components responsible for providing the structural support of tissue is proportional to the size of a land animal. For small animals like mice, it is about few percent. For humans, more than 1/10 of their body. For an elephant, the largest land animal on Earth, it is about 1/3 of their body.

For most marine mammals, the static scaling factor is comparable with the human one over a wide range of weights because the animal's weight is compensated by the buoyancy force exerted by water on immersed objects. However, gravity may have a significant effect on brain-blood flow and the location and size of internal organs in marine species, particularly on the most important of all: the heart.

The first time I thought about the impact of gravity on the human species was during my student days, when I participated in the Tien Shan mountaineering expedition. The remoteness of the sparsely populated mountain region from any centres of civilisation created significant logistical challenges. In order to provide a continuous supply of food and consumables during the expedition, we decided to create storages at a couple of points along our route. Prior to beginning the expedition, two small groups transported and stored deposits in the glacier's moraines where we could later collect them without significant deviation from the route.

After a Soviet military truck, Ural, dropped us off at the end of a dirt road we picked up the cargo and carried it on our shoulders for five kilometres. Each of us had our own rucksack full of belongings, including food and gear which weighed around 30kg (plus a 50kg box that was expected to be securely stored in glacier's moraine). Back then, the total weight of cargo could be compared to the weight of my own body. The bottom line is this was not an easy task. It took an entire day, from early morning to late evening, to cover these five kilometres. By the end of the journey, we were completely exhausted. Without the extra weight, it would take a person of our physical fitness no longer than an hour and a half.

During this walk, I was visited by a thought that I might feel a similar heaviness without cargo if I were on another planet with double the gravity. The next thought brought me some relief; on a planet with half the gravity, with that same load I would feel as if there was no extra-weight, even being able to run and jump. Unfortunately, people have no power over the laws of gravity. In that moment, on that journey, there was no other option but to continue with my heroic efforts to carry an abnormally heavy amount of weight.

Luckily, the lack of knowledge about the role of gravity in evolution cannot deprive us from the pleasure of speculating about the products of human evolution in two different environments, at double and half the gravity on planet Earth.

In the case of double the gravity, evolution would produce smaller and stockier hominids with dense, muscular bodies. They would be hairier to provide better thermal body insulation because of higher atmospheric convection. Higher gravity increases metabolic rate because an organism requires more energy for any kind of physical activity. That may reduce the life span of high gravity hominids. Is it just me, or do these creatures resemble gnomes or dwarfs from Western European fairy tales?

With half the gravity, hominids are expected to be taller, with longer necks, more slender bodies, and elongated limbs and fingers. Legs would be thinner and weaker, unless they were to be used for long distance leaps. Low gravity creatures may have smooth, almost hairless skin. Preferable ways of moving would be hopping or even flying. They may live longer lives. Don't these remind you of the elves in Lord of the Rings?

Who would win in a battle between armies of gnomes and elves on Earth? Based on my experience in Tien Shan, I would bet on gnomes because of their higher endurance at Earth's gravity and ability to wear heavy armours. One thing is for certain: neither of these armies would stand a chance in a battle against human longbow archers.

FIVE

SUPERFLUID WORLD

As you may have noticed, most of my imaginary travel destinations happen to be on celestial bodies that have only been visited or approached by robotic spaceships. This is because the knowledge gained through space missions and astronomical observations can help set scenes that are close to reality. The spice of realism creates an effect of presence, which makes imaginary journeys so thrilling that it's safe to say I have become addicted to them. There is one important exception in my collection of imaginary worlds. This special destination – superfluid world – is purely a product of my mind. The chances of its existence somewhere in our galaxy are vanishingly small. Why? To exist, this world would need to be even colder than 2.73K, the average temperature of Outer Space. Yet, no matter what I do, I cannot stop fantasising about the superfluid world because my imagination is generously fuelled by my long-term passion for superfluid helium.

I clearly remember the day I fell in love with this mysterious fluid. It happened during the first year of my PhD course. By this time, I'd already gained considerable experience in operating liquid helium based cryogenic equipment. Despite this, I'd never seen liquid helium with my own eyes because all cryostats and transport dewars were made of metal; unfortunately, normal humans cannot see through metal walls.

At the time, I was sharing a cryostat for my PhD project with my course mate, Oleg. A placement student, Vadim, was sharing our lab room too. Vadim was young and nice, full of curiosity, although a bit naïve for his age. His relentless bombarding of questions did, after some time, become annoying.

One day, when Oleg was transferring helium into the cryostat, Vadim, closely watching the procedure, innocently asked, "Oleg Igorevich what are you doing?" The extra-polite way of addressing older colleagues, using the patronymic name, was quite pleasant for us to hear. As young lads, we were just a few years older than Vadim and hardly worthy of such respect. The question caught Oleg, who was meditating on the helium level-meter's display, by surprise. His eyes moved to Vadim.

"Transferring liquid helium," answered Oleg apathetically. The vacant look on his face returned with no hesitation.

"Why are you so focused then? Is it because transferring helium could be dangerous?" asked Vadim, misinterpreting Oleg's facial impression.

The question suddenly sparked interest in Oleg's eyes and brought a blurred smile to his face. At that moment, I could already tell he had conceived an idea for a prank; in our department, Oleg had gained a reputation for being an enthusiastic prankster.

"Yes, Vadim, helium is quite an unpleasant liquid and you have to be very careful when transferring it," responded Oleg.

"What is liquid helium like?" Vadim questioned.

Oleg's eyes moved away from Vadim's face and stopped on a jar of strawberry jam on the shelf. "Helium is a dark-red, viscous, bad-smelling liquid."

Vadim gave him a sceptical look and loudly asked his micro-boss, Valeriy, who was sitting in the opposite corner of the lab, "Valeriy Borisovich, is it true?"

Valeriy, already following the dialogue, left his corner to get involved in the conversation. "Yes, Oleg is right; you have to be very careful. Just look at these terrible stains left on my lab gown by helium."

He pointed to a few dark spots on his brown lab gown, presumably left by pump oil. The answer left Vadim speechless for few minutes, abruptly terminating the chain of his helium related questions. Once Vadim left the room, we had a good laugh, after which Valeriy asked Oleg to reveal the prank to Vadim and educate him on the subject of liquid helium.

Almost a week later, Vadim volunteered to help me pick up a transport dewar from the helium liquefier hall. When we entered the hall, I smelled a strong stench of burned insulation mixed with the smell of solidol, a thick lubricant used in the Soviet era for lubricating various machines and devices. Vadim looked at me.

"Is this the smell of helium?" He asked.

I immediately realised that Oleg forgot about his promise.

After a sincere apology, Oleg promised me (again!) to start fulfilling his obligation immediately.

A few days later, our group leader Yuri Zakharovich (known also as Yu Z) informed all students of the department that he was going to perform a liquid helium demonstration in his precious, relict glass cryostat. Usually, Yu Z was very reluctant to use this historic piece of equipment, but Oleg managed to persuade him by referring to the noble purpose of educating the new generation of young physicists.

After a long meticulous preparation, Yu Z started the helium transfer. The attention of the group of observers, myself included, was focused on the inner glass vessel designed to host the liquid helium. The first splash of helium revealed a transparent and very turbulent liquid. It was boiling and swirling around the vessel like a powerful genie trapped in a bottle. Once the inner vessel was full, Yu Z disconnected the transfer syphon and started pumping out helium vapour. Crazy swirling gave place to intense boiling. Eventually, the temperature started dropping together with the level of the liquid. When the temperature approached 2.2K, the boiling intensified again and suddenly stopped just a moment later. This all came as a real shock to me. A few seconds prior, we were watching violent boiling. In that moment, I was looking at an absolutely quiet, perfectly clean and transparent liquid. Even in this quiet state, the surface of the liquid remained extremely sensitive to vibrations and mechanical noise.

"What you can see is the superfluid helium," commented Yu Z.

And that was it. That was the moment I fell in love with superfluid helium for the rest of my life.

During the demonstration Vadim and the other younger students learned that helium has no smell. If inhaled as a gas, helium changes the pitch of your voice in a way that sounds like the voice of a cartoon character. They also learned that superfluid helium has no viscosity and its thermal conductivity increases millions of times. Though I already knew the facts, I realised it is one thing to possess information and another thing to see it with your own eyes.

The word "superfluidity" contains a reference to its remarkable property: the ability of a liquid to flow without friction or viscosity. However, it is only one of a few characteristics of Bose Einstein condensation, the fundamental phenomenon that can be observed in different physical systems. Explaining Bose Einstein condensate is not an easy task and I am not confident that I can do it without the risk of the topic sounding ambiguous and, as a sad result, boring, so I invite you to visit the ***Parallel Thought 5.1*** for more reflections.

For years, the superfluidity of helium had a very positive reputation as a fruitful research subject in the low temperature physics community. At the same time, it is a state of helium, which is the most hated fluid by cryogenic engineers who design and operate ultra-low temperature refrigerators that have become indispensable for cooling various bits of scientific equipment such as quantum computers or dark-matter detectors. The root of this hatred lies in the ability of superfluid helium to escape from sealed vessels through the tiniest leaks into the vacuum space of cryostats. Such leaks ruin a cryostat's thermal insulation.

Let's now return to the astronomical body in the form of a small planet or asteroid far away from stars or other heat sources. Such a location should keep the planet's temperature quite cold, just a few Kelvin. Using the unlimited power of our imagination, let's pour out enough liquid helium to cover the whole surface of the planet with a shallow ocean. Immediately after that, the helium would start to evaporate into the vacuum of space, cooling itself and the surface of the planet. With any luck, there could be some liquid left in the craters and dimples after the temperature of the liquid helium drops below 2.17K, the temperature of superfluid transition.

The final scene of our imaginary journey is now almost complete. Before we can start exploring this world, we need to sort out the lighting problem. Let me remind you that the planet of our interest is far away from any star; we are in near total darkness. Any attempt to use conventional light sources could lead to heat and may create temperature gradients that are best to avoid (I will explain why a little later). One possible solution is a pair of night vision goggles with a sufficient sensitivity range to detect scattered light from the alien landscape illuminated by stars in the night sky or by another very gentle light source.

It is also worth saying a few words about the spacesuit that would be expected to be worn in this world. In this particular case, it would need to be very special, because none of the known spacesuit technologies would provide sufficient thermal insulation from the superfluid helium environment. In order to achieve a reasonable level of insulation, we need to create a suit like an anti-cryostat with a super-leak-tight vacuum space between the inner and outer shells. With our current level of technology, this could only be achieved if the whole suit were made of metal, preferably stainless steel. To allow our limbs movement, we'd need to incorporate sections made of soft bellows. All the joints between the suit's components would need to be either welded or connected by vacuum flanges bolted together. In principle, this is possible. In reality, I have a strong suspicion that this would be an extremely uncomfortable costume. One that would make the armour of a medieval knight look like loungewear.

Enough of that. Let's pretend the vision and insulation problems are sorted, so we can surrender to the pleasure of exploring this bizarre place. *The world we are expecting to see is a dark, colourless place without a distinctive smell. The reason I touch on the subject of smell is because humans can breathe helium gas if it's mixed with 21% oxygen (which we have to supply ourselves). Such a mixture is also known as "heliox" and used in medical treatments for patients who have difficulty breathing. The only significant consequence of heliox breathing is the pitch change in our voice, making humans sound like cartoon characters. In this world, the sky is expected to be quite dull, without bright stars, moons or planets. Even if there were to be a massive astronomical object nearby, it would be pitch black and, as a result, almost invisible in the sky.*

Now that we've had a period of initial reflection, let's start active exploration. We should start from the most obvious trial: walking into a shallow puddle of superfluid helium at the bottom of a small crater right in front of us. As we slowly step into the puddle, after a few steps we would experience the first surprise; if we move slowly enough, we wouldn't feel resistance from the liquid, nor would we see the liquid disturbed by our motion. It would be like there was no liquid there at all.

If we walk faster and faster, we'd get to a point where we would start to feel liquid resistance. At this point, we would have exceeded the Landau critical velocity. We will return to

Lev Landau and his enigmatic two-fluid model later. Above this velocity, liquid helium does not behave like a superfluid and liquid's viscosity is no longer zero.

If we were to take a closer look at the superfluid liquid around our legs, we would realise that each energetic leg movement leaves behind a number of vortexes. Despite the similarity to ordinary vortexes in water on first inspection, the nature of vortices in superfluid helium is very different. Any rotational motion of a superfluid is sustained by quantized vortices. As a result, the quantized vortex is a stable topological defect and, once created, should persist without decay forever. The idea of quantized vortices belonged to Norwegian physicist Lars Onsager and was later developed by the brilliant American theoretician, Richard Feynman. The main consequence of this for our walk would be the trace of quantized vortexes left behind us. To create vortexes, our leg should move faster than vortex generating velocity. We should generate a critical velocity of around 1 m/s, which is two orders of magnitude smaller than

the critical velocity theoretically predicted by Landau. All in all, if we do not want to be traced walking across the superfluid helium lake, we'd need to move at a slow pace, not allowing our legs to create quantized vortexes in superfluid helium.

Such reflection makes me think about a bizarre cryo-space sport: racing in a superfluid lake. To participate in such a challenge, one would need to cross the lake without generating a single quantized vortex, which would be very easy to detect in the superfluid liquid. This would no doubt be a tough competition; moving legs at optimal speed in an uncomfortable super-leak-tight spacesuit would require an extremely high level of body control.

For our next virtual experiment, we need a super-leak-tight bucket. First, we submerge the whole bucket to fill it up with superfluid liquid. Then we pull it out and hold it just above the surface of the pond. Almost instantly, liquid helium would start to seep out through the bottom of the bucket and back into the pond. Hold on! If we agreed that there are no leaks, how would liquid helium escape from the bucket? The only reasonable explanation would be if the liquid, defying gravity, climbed up the walls and over the bucket's edge, rushing back down into the pond. The idea of upward flowing liquid might sound supernatural, but this is exactly the sort of phenomenon that would happen with superfluid helium. Despite the strong temptation to give you a detailed explanation, I better stop myself here. After all, I am not sure the extent to which you share my excitement of this bizarre behaviour. To avoid running the risk of sounding boring, let me instead invite you to **Parallel Thought 5.2.** There is another spectacular demonstration of uphill flowing superfluid helium: the superfluid fountain effect. However, to demonstrate this phenomenon, we may need to do a little bit of DIY, which is described in **Parallel Thought 5.3.**

The extraordinary ability of superfluid helium to overtake obstacles kills the concepts of artificial barriers designed to hold liquid, such as dams, canal locks and irrigation constructions like ditches and reservoirs. Why would we need such structures in this weird world in the first place?

Before we start our imaginary demonstration, we need to submerge the bottom end of the tube into superfluid helium. For clarity it would be better to hold the tube slightly tilted from the vertical position. To start the demo, we would need to direct a laser beam onto the part of the tube occupied by compressed powder. As soon as the laser beam hits the tube's surface, we should see the jet of liquid helium escaping from the nozzle. Voila! Enjoy a superfluid fountain. If we switch off the pointer, the jet quickly disappears. If switched on again, the jet is back in full swing. The most amazing thing about the superfluid fountain is that it is driven only by temperature gradient; in other words, the heat is directly transformed into mechanical work, which is the reason the phenomenon is also known as the thermomechanical effect.

I don't know about you, but all these strange properties of superfluid helium encourage me to consider the possibility of virtual swimming in superfluid liquid. If this were possible, it makes our imaginary swim in Titan's lake look like an extremely dull experience. Unfortunately, an undefeatable obstacle nips this idea in the bud. The reason for this is the extremely low density of liquid helium, which is $1/8^{th}$ the density of water and less than two times denser than liquid hydrogen (the lightest liquid known). Taking 62L (the average volume of a human body) as an example, one would need to displace 500L (half a cubic meter!) of liquid helium just to make it float near the surface completely submerged into the liquid. This condition could be satisfied for a weightless zorb ball, one metre in diameter, which encapsulates the body. However, as soon as we take into account the weight of a super-leak proof double-walled zorb made of 5mm thick glass, plus the weight of air at ambient conditions inside the zorb, the diameter would need to increase to 1.3m. Finally, if we would like to be less than half-submerged, to see what is happening above and below the surface, the diameter can easily reach two metres. I'm afraid this makes any kind of "Michelin" suit, similar to the one we used for swimming in Titan lakes, utterly unrealistic. Nevertheless, floating in a glass zorb has every promise of being a marvellous experience.

Let's place ourselves into a glass zorb ball of 2m diameter equipped with a life support system which supplies oxygen for breathing and controls the temperature inside the vessel to stay comfortable. Initially we wouldn't feel anything strange; even if we attempted a gentle jump, the zorb would react in the same way it would on the surface of ordinary water. Disturbed by our abrupt movement, it starts swaying in a vertical direction. Fairly soon afterward, we sense that something strange is happening. Whilst a water zorb would stop moving after a few fading oscillations, in superfluid helium the zorb would continue to sway without any sign of stopping. If the temperature of liquid helium remains around or below 1K, this swaying would continue for a long time. The same would happen if we were to spin the zorb; the spinning would continue for days, years or maybe even centuries. This is down to the very small friction between the moving zorb and the superfluid helium. This friction is temperature dependant; just below the superfluid transition, the zorb's spinning would slow down much faster than at lower temperatures.

This strange behaviour has been explained by the two-fluid model developed by Soviet theoretician Lev Landau. According to the model, superfluid helium consists of two interpenetrating fluid components: superfluid and normal. The superfluid component has no viscosity and does not interact with the moving surface of the zorb's wall. The normal component is an ordinary liquid with viscosity and other properties inherent to ordinary liquids. At the superfluid transition of 2.17K, the normal component is 100%. As the temperature decreases, the normal component declines and superfluid increases. At around 1K and below the normal component fraction is negligibly small; almost the entire liquid consists of the superfluid component. I know this mathematical abstraction seems very odd, but the model nicely describes the reality. If the temperature of the lake is around 1K we may need longer than a human lifetime to notice even the tiniest deceleration in the zorb's rotation. *I believe that after a few minutes this experience would become a bit boring. After spending half an hour in the rotating zorb in the middle of a superfluid helium lake, we would be very happy to return home to a cosy sofa and a quiet period of reflection.* After a few minutes, it'd seem like the perfect time to put the kettle on to make a nice cup of tea: milk and one sugar.

PARALLEL THOUGHT 5.1
BOSE EINSTEIN CONDENSATE

As temperature decreases, most substances undergo a phase transition and become solid. There are, however, a few exceptions. One is helium, which remains liquid until absolute zero. There are also other examples to which I will return later on.

At extremely low temperatures, everything is governed by laws of quantum mechanics that radically differ from the laws of classical physics responsible for dictating the physical world we experience in everyday life. Quantum mechanics does not allow things like elementary particles or atoms to have any amount of energy; their energy comes in discrete levels, which means particles can stay at different energy levels, but never in between these levels. Though this is actually always true, at room temperature, other larger energy scale processes outweigh the quantum effects.

There are two different rules of populating energy levels. One is called **Bose–Einstein statistics** developed by Satyendra Nath Bose and expanded later by Albert Einstein. Another is **Fermi–Dirac statistics** named after Enrico Fermi and Paul Dirac, each of whom developed the model independently.

Before we look at quantum statistics in more details, I need to say few words about the particle spin. In quantum mechanics, spin is an intrinsic property of all elementary particles. All known particles that constitute ordinary matter such as electrons, neutrons and protons have half-integer spin of ½. They obey the Fermi–Dirac statistics and are called fermions. Any particles with integer values of spin that obey Bose–Einstein statistics are named bosons.

For example, the helium-4 atom – which consists of two protons, two neutrons and two electrons – has all spins oppositely aligned, which makes the total spin 0. For that reason, the helium-4 atom obeys the Bose–Einstein statistics and called boson.

On the contrary, another stable isotope, helium-3, is missing one neutron and consequently the total spin is half-integer. That makes the helium-3 atom a fermion, which strongly influences its behaviour at extremely low temperatures. More about that later.

There is a fundamental difference between the two types of quantum statistics. The Bose–Einstein statistics allow multiple boson occupancy of the same state. Contrarily, the Fermi–Dirac statistics require particles to obey the "Pauli exclusion principle" proposed by Austrian theoretical physicist Wolfgang Pauli. The principle states that two or more identical fermions cannot occupy the same quantum state simultaneously.

If we cool a gas of weakly interacting bosons very close to absolute zero, at some point a significant number of particles will occupy the lowest quantum state, in which they become mathematically indistinguishable and start to behave coherently. These particles stop bumping into each other and start to ignore local imperfections like impurities or walls of the container. The accumulation of bosons on the lowest quantum level is known as Bose Einstein Condensation (BEC). The BEC of helium atoms turns helium-4 into superfluid liquid.

Both the Soviet physicist Pyotr Kapitsa and the British

duo John Allen and Don Misener have independently discovered the superfluidity of helium-4 in experiments which involve helium flow through a tiny gap between a pair of glass disks. In these experiments, the viscosity was so low that Kapitsa coined the term "superfluidity" by analogy to "superconductivity" which is, by the way, another example of BEC happening in a liquid of electrons. I'm very aware I just told you that electrons are fermions, meaning they cannot accumulate on the same lowest energy level and then form BEC. Cracking this puzzle has won a trio of theorists – John Bardeen, Leon Cooper, and John Robert Schrieffer – a Nobel Prize. Fun fact, this was John Bardeen's second Nobel Prize; the first was awarded for the invention of the transistor.

In metals, electrons exist as a gas of free particles filling a space in between ions that form a rigid lattice of metal. Electrons are repelled from each other because of their negative charge, but they are also attracted to positively charged ions. At low temperatures, the interplay between repulsion and attraction forces can pair electrons together, forming so-called Cooper pairs. Think of a pair of dancers doing a waltz, maintaining more or less the same distance from each other whilst spinning. The total spin of such pair is an integer. Now, as a gas of composite bosons, they can form BEC and remain in this extraordinary state as long as the waltz continues uninterrupted. The forces that keep electrons paired are quite weak, so the thermal energy can easily break the pairs. That explains why accumulating a significant number of Cooper pairs, enough for forming BEC, requires low temperatures.

A similar transformation happens with helium-3 atoms, which, as explained above, are also fermions. At sub-Kelvin temperatures, helium-3 behaves as a viscous Fermi-liquid, but below 0.00265K (almost 1,000 times lower than the temperature of superfluid transition in helium-4), the helium-3 atoms form Cooper pairs and the superfluid transition occurs.

There are few more systems where BEC could happen. The closest to the ideal theoretical model of BEC happens to be BEC of ultra-cold atoms accumulated in optical traps. In this case, the atomic vapour is so dilute that interaction between individual atoms is negligible, providing a sample of nearly pure condensate. For comparison, the liquid like interaction between helium-4 atoms limits the Bose-Einstein condensate fraction to somewhere between 7 and 8 %.

Finally, the most incredible object where BEC is expected to happen is a neutron star: the collapsed core of massive star that exploded as supernovae. The extremely high pressure inside neutron stars squeezes neutrons so tightly that a teaspoonful of the matter would weigh billions of tonnes. Thanks to this enormous pressure, there is a possibility of BEC formation despite extremely high temperatures inside neutron stars. However, in fairness, we do not yet know enough about these enigmatic heavenly bodies to make any credible conclusion regarding the processes happening inside them.

PARALLEL THOUGHT 5.2

SUPERFLUID HELIUM ESCAPING FROM BUCKET

All liquids form thin films that climb up vertical wettable surfaces. The transport is driven by the Van der Waals force if it is higher than gravity. Only two processes can either stop or slow down the climbing: viscosity (or internal friction) and evaporation of the liquid. In the case of low saturated vapour pressure, the liquid can travel for a surprisingly long distance. A good example is an oily film that covers the surface of a bottle. No matter how tightly the bottle cork is closed, the bottle is always oily to the touch if it has been opened.

Liquid helium wets almost all known substances except some alkali metals. The saturated pressure of superfluid helium is quite low; if we are not far from thermodynamic equilibrium, the helium evaporation is negligible. In our virtual demonstration, the key is in the frictionless flow of superfluid liquid. Thus, the superfluid film quickly climbs up the vertical wall, reaches the bucket's upper rim and rushes down along the outer wall accelerated by gravity. The process is so intense that superfluid helium can disappear from the bucket before our very eyes.

The ability of superfluid liquids to cross obstacles that lie at a higher level is also known as Onnes effect, named after Dutch physicist Heike Kamerlingh Onnes, who liquefied helium for the first time in a 1908 experiment.

PARALLEL THOUGHT 5.3.

DIY DEVICE FOR SUPERFLUID HELIUM FOUNTAIN

1. Begin with a stainless-steel tube with thin wall (10cm long and 10mm in diameter).
2. Take a piece of cotton wool and squeeze it into smaller, denser ball and shove it into the tube, using the tail of a 9mm drill as a pushing piston. We may need to insert two or more balls to form a plug, which noticeably resist pushing.
3. Push the plug about 3cm deep into the tube.
4. Take a quarter teaspoon of fine powder, crocus would do, and pour it into the tube's end plugged with cotton wool, tamping it by drill's tail. This should occupy about 1cm of the tube's length.
5. Close the tube with another cotton wool plug to prevent powder spilling out. The bottom end of the device is finished.
6. Squeeze the opposite end with pliers leaving a 2mm gap between the flattened tube walls.
7. Clamp two corners of the flattened end, leaving an orifice of about 2mm. That should form a nice nozzle on the upper end of the tube (opposite to the one stuffed with powder).
8. The device is now ready for use. For our demonstration we would also need a standard class 3A Laser Pointer.

EPILOGUE

I'm sure it wasn't a surprise that the Superfluid World chapter went beyond what is reasonable in its weirdness. My best excuse is that it was written during Covid-19 lockdown, an odd time which allowed my imagination to run wilder than ever. The extreme nature of this chapter is also supposed to be somewhat of a grand finale of the imaginary tour through the outer cryo worlds.

Why, then, do I get a feeling that my mission is yet to be accomplished?

I have experienced this feeling before, as a child, whenever I shared my collection of stamps (badges, minerals and later vinyl records) with a new friend. It usually started from the crown jewel of my collection – here, it is definitely the cryo world of Titan; back then it was whichever mundane item was most valuable – but after that I just could not stop and had to keep going until the very last item was revealed. We are now in a similar situation, somewhere in between the second and third stage of this collection sharing. To accomplish our journey, I invite you to scan through the remaining items of my outer cryo-worlds collection which, for one reason or another, did not make it into the main part of the book.

Let us start from the fiery Mercury: the planet that has absolutely nothing to do with cryo-worlds at first glance. Due to its close proximity to the Sun, the temperature at the surface of Mercury is searing, easily reaching 700K (427°C). That's about 100°C above the melting point of lead, which would form liquid lakes if it existed on Mercury in large quantities. However, the absence of an atmosphere creates a steep temperature gradient between the equator and the poles; therefore, the temperature in Polar Regions never exceeds 180K. Moreover, at the floors of deep polar craters, which are never exposed to direct sunlight, the temperature could remain around 100K. It was at the North Pole craters where instruments of the Messenger spacecraft discovered the presence of ice made up of water in 2012. The mission's principal investigator, Sean Solomon, estimated the volume of ice to be large enough to "encase Washington D.C. in a frozen block two and a half miles deep", as quoted to *The New York Times*. Mercury is, quite literally, the planet of "ice and fire". These cryogenic conditions certainly satisfy our criteria for outer cryo-worlds. However, there is one serious obstacle for using this place as a destination for our imaginary journeys: Mercury receives the most intense solar radiation of all the planets in the Solar System. The level is so high that even a short walk inside the polar crater could be deadly for a human.

Paradoxically, we can find similar conditions – without the deadly radiation – much closer to home. On our own natural satellite, the Moon, ice deposits were found in permanently shadowed craters on the North and South poles. Thanks to the deep darkness, absence of an atmosphere and much longer distance from the Sun, the bottoms of polar craters on the Moon are extremely cold. The Diviner Lunar Radiometer installed on Lunar Reconnaissance Orbiter, launched in 2009, measured 26K in the north polar crater Hermite, the coldest temperature ever measured by a spacecraft, colder even than the surface of Pluto. Therefore, in possession of the coldest spot in the Solar System, the Moon deserves the coolest place in the "Outer Cryo-Worlds" club. You might be asking, why then did I not dedicate one of the chapters to the Moon? The reason is this: all the videos and pictures of Apollo missions in combination with the vast knowledge collected by scientists might make our imaginary journey to the Moon a mundane exercise. Imagine a virtual tour to the International Space Station: interesting, but not that exciting, at least not for me.

The next fascinating item in the outer cryo-world collection is Jupiter's satellite, Ganymede. The biggest satellite in the Solar System, the Ganymede is in many ways similar to other Galilean moons such as Io, Europa and Callisto. It might even have a liquid water ocean under the icy surface. There are, however, a few interesting features. One of them, a chain of craters named Enki Catena, has captured my imagination. The 13 overlapping craters follow an almost perfect straight line. There is a theory that the gigantic chain might be formed by fragments of a comet pulled to pieces by Jupiter's gravity, when they crashed onto Ganymede in quick succession. The most interesting feature is the thin atmosphere on Ganymede, which consists almost entirely of oxygen. The oxygen is supposed to be created when the cosmic radiation hits the water ice on the moon's surface and knocks out the hydrogen. Eventually, light hydrogen escapes into space leaving the oxygen behind. A similar process might also be behind the oxygen-rich atmosphere on Europa. This makes the atmospheres of Ganymede and Europa potentially breathable for humans, of course under the condition that the density of the gas increases millions of times by compression. When taking the first breath of Ganymede's air once this technical problem is resolved, I would expect a pungent smell: ozone. The odour is reminiscent of chlorine and the familiar smell of an approaching storm. Ozone could be detectable at very low concentrations, as little as 0.1 part per million in air. In Ganymede's atmosphere it is expected to be produced from molecular oxygen under exposure to ultraviolet and x-rays that irradiate the surface of the moon. One needs to be careful when breathing Ganymede's air because high levels of exposure to ozone may cause headaches, coughs and shortness of breath. Based on the foregoing, my guess is a virtual walk down the Enki Catena craters chain, breathing Ganymede's smelly air would be quite an enjoyable adventure, but do not forget about the fact that you're also pushing a trolley with a huge turbo-molecular pump and battery in front of you.

The next brief stop is the dwarf planet Ceres, previously mentioned in the Cryovolcanoes chapter. Ceres is the largest object in the Asteroid Belt positioned between the orbits of Mars and Jupiter. Its long distance from the Sun defines its temperature range, which extends from 130K at night to

200K during the day. In general, the surface of Ceres has quite low reflectivity, like worn tarmac, but there are a few shimmering spots. The brightest spot has been observed by Dawn spacecraft (launched by NASA in 2007) in the middle of a crater called Occator. The high brightness of this and other similar features might be caused by a substance on the surface that effectively reflects sunlight. At present, the composition and origin of the substance are not clearly understood, but inch thick layers of coarse-grained rhinestone crystals might provide comparable reflectivity.

Let's now move our imagination to the rim of the crater Occator. We are in a spacesuit, looking down to the crater interior. From the height of the ridge, we can clearly see the edge of a shining area, somewhere in the centre of crater, around 20km away. We fearlessly jump down the slope and start our journey towards it. Do not worry about the jump; the gravity on Ceres' surface is six times smaller than on the Moon, which in turn is six times smaller than on the Earth. Once we reach the crater's bottom we can continue moving in long leaps, like on the Moon, but even longer. Thanks to the absence of atmosphere and very low gravity, this moonwalk (or rather moon-run) should allow us to move faster than a marathon runner. We can also try moon-hopping, just for fun. The journey to the outer edge of the shining area would take no longer than an hour. However, if you do not like physical challenges, you could use a jetpack, similar to the well-known Flyboard Air created and operated by Franky Zapata. On Ceres, the jetpack would need to be more than 30 times less powerful. Using a jetpack, we could cover the distance in just a few minutes.

Approaching the edge of the shining area is expected to be the most spectacular part of our journey. The intensity of light reflected from the glimmering substance would be so high that it might even get uncomfortable to look at. Thanks to the smart-visor of spacesuit helmet, the sunglass-like filters are activated automatically as soon as dangerous levels of brightness are detected. Now we can gently land to the glittering ground and explore the surrounding area. At the moment we do not know what the bright spot would look like in close proximity. It may look like a snowfield or one of these salt flats formed by dried-up lakes. One thing I am sure about is that the texture of the surface should be rather different from the normal Ceres terrain. Another interesting feature of the bright spot is the temperature of the shining substance is expected to be lower than on the rest of the dwarf planet because it would absorb less sunlight, and heat up less as a result.

Let's now leave the enigmatic bright spot on Ceres and shift our attention to the three tiny celestial bodies famous for their unusual shape: Hyperion, Pan and Arrokoth.

Saturn's moon Hyperion looks like a gigantic potato-shaped sponge, or a wasp nest. It was the first discovered moon with a non-round shape. The low density of this chaotically rotating moon suggests that it is mainly composed of ice, a small amount of rock and many voids; however, the process responsible for such a unique structure remains unexplained. The average temperature on Hyperion is 90K, so substances like water, carbon dioxide and most of the hydrocarbons are frozen.

The shape of another of Saturn's moon, Pan, is even more captivating. For many Pan has the appearance of a 30km long ravioli; for me, it rather resembles a gargantuan Siberian pelmeni. This moon is approximately 10 times smaller than Hyperion and its surface is slightly colder. Pan is a ring-shepherd and is responsible for keeping the Encke Gap within the A ring free of particles that may range from grains of sand to mountain-size chunks.

The Kuiper Belt object, Arrokoth, previously nicknamed Ultima Thule before its official naming, is shaped like a 36km tall gingerbread man. NASA's New Horizons spacecraft visited it in 2019. The average temperature on Arrokoth is estimated to be around 40K with a maximum of 60K on the area illuminated by the Sun. This could be the coolest giant gingerbread man in our Solar System.

All three objects have one common feature, which makes the imaginary exploration rather attractive. All are tiny in terms of celestial body size and as a result have extremely low gravity, which is 500 times smaller on Hyperion and 10,000 times smaller on Pan and Arrokoth than on Earth. The only thing we need for exploring these worlds is a spacesuit designed for spacewalks. After a gentle push off the ground, we can fly above the surface for minutes or even hours. The strength of the push should be carefully calculated. Too intense and we could attain the sort of cosmic velocity that would send us on an escape trajectory from the gravitational field of the object and into open space. The risk of such escape is much higher for Pan and Arrokoth because their gravity is about 20 times smaller than on Hyperion. For comfortable exploration, I would recommend using the Manned Manoeuvring Unit, a propulsion unit used by the Space Shuttle astronauts to perform unstrapped extravehicular spacewalks at a distance from the shuttle. Then we can adjust our trajectory in a way that would allow us to levitate just above the surface and choose the distance and direction of our flight. If I were to pick a personal favourite, it would be the flight above Pan because the complex view on Pan, Saturn and its A ring with the gap promises the most breathtaking scenery imaginable.

The level of gravity on Hyperion creates a possibility for yet another weird space sport, one I'd like to call Hyperion golf. As it happens, the values of Hyperion's radius and gravity give an estimation of the escape velocity at around 70 meters per second, while the maximum speed record for a golf ball is 94 meters per second. The aim of Hyperion golf would be to hit a small ball so that it orbits the moon for as long as possible before dropping back to the ground. Any participant whose ball escapes into open space would be out of the competition. Hence, a successful Hyperion golfer would need to be very good at launching the ball in an optimal trajectory at the right speed. This may be complicated even further by the necessity to wear an uncomfortable space suit. The ultimate winner would be the golfer who manages to launch the ball to a stable orbit.

There is one aspect of Earth golf that notably reduces the environmental friendliness of this sport. I believe all of us have seen bright white golf balls scattered around golf courses often integrated into picturesque nature conservation areas. The problem is that golf balls are made of tough, non-degradable plastic and could remain in the environment for hundreds of years. In the case of Hyperion golf, we can easily avoid this unsustainable contamination by making balls out of frozen water. In Hyperion's low temperature environment, the ice would be as strong as stainless steel, a good material of choice for the ball. The moon already largely consists of ice; adding a few more balls will not change the ecological situation a drastic amount.

Finally, we are approaching the weirdest item of the collection: the first known interstellar object named Oumuamua. For a long time, astronomers suspected that this class of celestial bodies should exist but had never seen one such interstellar object passing through the Solar System. It came out of dark from the approximate direction of the star Vega in the northern constellation of Lyra. Interestingly, Oumuamua travelled undetected through the Solar System at a blistering speed until it passed the Sun, where it was observed for the first time in October 2017 by the University of Hawaii's Pan-STARRS 1 telescope. Everything related to Oumuamua is puzzling. Originally, it was classified as a comet, but when new observations found no signs of cometary activity it was briefly reclassified as an asteroid. This didn't last long; following measurements revealed that it was slightly accelerating, more like a comet again. The shape of the interstellar object was also unique. It looked like a gigantic 400-meter-long cigar, with a width spanning tens of metres. There is no other known astronomical body of this shape in the Solar System. Oumuamua does not fly in a stable projectile like the Starship Enterprise; instead, it spins on its axis every 7.3 hours. The only expected property of Oumuamua is the deep red colour, quite common for objects from the outskirts of the Solar System.

Scientists suggest that Oumuamua was wandering the Milky Way for hundreds of millions of years before it passed by the Solar System. It is now speeding toward the constellation Pegasus at a staggering speed of 44 kilometres per second with respect to the Sun. Soon, it will disappear forever into the coldness of interstellar space.

Whilst the enigmatic Oumuamua is the last outer cryo-world object we will look at, my current collection is far from complete. There are myriads of cryo-worlds out there that we do not know much about. However, this area of knowledge is rapidly expanding thanks to new space missions. Actually, in the very near future, we may learn things which could fundamentally change our perception of celestial bodies in the Solar System. That will also provide us with a lot of fresh food for imagination. If you are interested in future missions that promise to quench the thirst for news related to outer cryo worlds, you are welcome to visit *Parallel Thought E.1*.

Let's not forget about another, more traditional window into outer worlds: astronomy observations. Thanks to the rapid development of telescope technology, modern observatories compete on equal terms with space robots in providing breath-taking images to both academia and mass media. I am going to discuss this area of space exploration in *Parallel Thought E.2*.

To end on an optimistic note feels like a fine place to end. Before I disappear from your mind, however, I would like to apologise a final time for those occasions when I stretched my fantasy beyond the reasonable. I know how frustrating it can be to read without being offered the chance to argue your point directly with the book's author, especially if you have a strong opinion. Therefore, I promise to be easily available for debate in the virtual space of the internet and it will always be a great pleasure to discuss the wonderful and endlessly fascinating topic of outer cryo worlds with you.

PARALLEL THOUGHT E.1
FUTURE SPACE MISSIONS

Recent explosion of public interest in celestial bodies has attracted significant financial and technical resources for space exploration that is about to bear fruit. Quite a few missions are already in their final stages of preparation and many more are under consideration.

Let's start from the extravaganza of Mars exploration missions which are occurring now or going to happen in the nearest future. Three robotic spacecrafts are already heading towards Mars and are going to be joined by another within a couple of years. There are extremely high expectations for all of them.

I would like to start from NASA's Mars van-sized robot rover called Perseverance, which left Earth on July 30th 2020 on a mission to try and detect life on Mars. On February 18th, after "the seven minutes of terror" Perseverance has successfully landed on Mars. In these seven minutes Perseverance decelerated in upper Martian atmosphere from mind-blowing 20000 km/hr to about tenth of this speed using heatshield. Then supersonic parachute reduced its speed further to a few hundred kilometres per hour this was still too fast for a safe landing. So it cut itself loose from the parachute and used rocket thrusters to slow down and stop its descent at just 20 metres above the Martian ground then it was gently lowered to the surface by rocket platform called "sky crane".

Following the successful lending, the six-wheeled rover will look for signs of ancient life in a large Martian crater called Jezero, which in several Slavic languages means 'lake'. The crater thought to host once an ancient lake and it contains a fan-delta deposit rich in clays that may contain signs of past life. Perseverance is carrying a suite of scientific instruments designed to sample and analyse Martian soil for bio-signatures – chemical markers of life.

The most interesting samples of terrain will be stored in metal canisters and left behind on the Martian surface. Sometime after 2026, ESA will send a "fetch rover" to Mars that will travel across the surface picking up canisters left behind by Perseverance. The canisters will be loaded into a protective container and placed into a small rocket called Mars Ascent Vehicle that will deliver the container into orbit around Mars. The sample container will then be met in orbit and transferred onto a European cargo ship, which will bring the samples back to Earth. If everything goes according to plan, it is expected that the capsule with samples will land in North America around 2031.

In addition to the equipment required for detecting life – 23 cameras, a few spectrometers, microphone and drill – there are a number of unusual objects too, such as a tiny piece of Martian meteorite (to be used for the calibration of rover's instruments), or a few samples of spacesuit materials to monitor the impact of the harsh Martian environment on them. Another example is an on-board device which will attempt to make oxygen from the carbon dioxide-dominated atmosphere, important technology for future human exploration. Perseverance will also carry a tiny robot helicopter, Ingenuity, which will test the new technology and help to plan the best driving route for Mars rovers.

The equally ambitious Chinese Tianwen-1, or "Questions

to Heaven", mission consists of a robotic spaceship that will orbit Mars, a lander and a rover that will travel across the Martian surface in search of water. The spaceship was lifted off Earth by a Long March 5 rocket on July 23rd 2020. It has arrived in orbit around the Red Planet in February 2021.

There is also the Hope mission: an unusual collaboration between the United Arab Emirates and Japan. It was successfully launched from Tanegashima spaceport on a Japanese H-2A rocket on July 19th 2020 and reached Mars on 9 February 2021 when the spacecraft entered into an orbit around the Red Planet making the UAE the first Arab nation in history to have a scientific presence at Earth's near neighbour. The craft already returned its first picture of Mars and is expected to study the Martian weather and climate in detail.

The joint ESA and Roscosmos ExoMars lander mission scheduled in 2022 will deploy the Rosalind Franklin rover to the surface of Mars. It will carry a two-metre subsurface sampling drill and an onboard analytical laboratory. Once safely landed, the solar powered rover will travel across the Martian terrane to search for biomolecules or bio-signatures from past life.

In any case, we can expect a great number of astonishing pictures and videos (probably even in 3D) because all rovers and spaceships are equipped with cutting-edge, high-resolution cameras.

Despite the current hive of activity caused by the launch and operation of numerous Martian spaceships, the space exploration community does not stop efforts aimed at considering and planning future interplanetary missions.

One of the most developed NASA missions of this kind

is the Europa Clipper, set for launch in 2024. During a series of flybys while orbiting Jupiter the robotic spacecraft will investigate the Galilean moon that may have conditions suitable for life. By the way, this is not the only Europa-focused mission in NASA's portfolio. The space agency is also working on the Europa Lander concept as a potential future mission that would look for signs of life on the moon's icy surface material.

NASA researchers have also proposed a similar mission to Neptune's moon Triton. I did not mention Triton in this book because too little is known about this dark, freezing world but, like Europa, it may host an ocean of liquid water beneath its icy crust.

Of course, space researchers did not forget about Titan; how could they? Recently NASA has announced the Dragonfly mission that is expected to be launched in 2027 and arrive on Titan in 2035. Once orbiting Titan, the spacecraft will deploy a large drone on the surface of the moon. The eight-rotor drone will take advantage of Titan's dense atmosphere to fly from one place to another where it will study various surface materials. The mission's focus is on prebiotic chemical processes common on both Titan and Earth. I have no doubt that numerous high-resolution pictures sent by Dragonfly drone and video broadcast streamed live from Titan's terrane will blow our imagination.

PARALLEL THOUGHT E.2
FUTURE OF ASTRONOMY OBSERVATION

A robotic spacecraft is not the only window into the outer worlds. Recent rapid developments in the technology of telescopes opens up new horizons for space exploration. Most modern telescopes allow observation of celestial bodies with unprecedented resolution and are capable of producing highly detailed images on a broad spectrum. Today, the superhero of astronomy is undoubtedly NASA's Hubble Space Telescope. Its achievements in the exploration of outer cryo worlds are difficult to overestimate. Hubble observed evidence of transient changes in the atmosphere above the surface of Jupiter's moon, Europa, that might be caused by gas plumes expelled from a subsurface ocean. Hubble also provided the best evidence yet for an underground saltwater ocean on Ganymede by detecting related activity in Ganymede's own auroras. The telescope is still operational and could last until 2040. However, ageing takes its toll and quite a few important functions are currently disabled due to technical problems. NASA's successor to the Hubble telescope is the James Webb Space Telescope, which is scheduled for launch in March 2021.

The Herschel Space Observatory built and operated by ESA was active from 2009 to 2013, a much shorter time than the Hubble. Nonetheless, it was enough time to make a few remarkable discoveries that are relevant to our subject. For example, Herschel has shown that the water expelled from the moon Enceladus fissures near its south pole, known as the Tiger Stripes, forms a giant ring around Saturn. The data from Herschel also made possible the detection of water vapour on the dwarf planet Ceres in 2014, a discovery that came before the arrival of NASA's Dawn mission at Ceres.

Strictly speaking, Webb seems more like Herschel on steroids rather than an advanced version of Hubble. Like Herschel, Webb will look at the universe in infrared, while Hubble studies it in optical and ultraviolet bands. In any case, Webb will have a 6.5-meter diameter primary mirror, much larger than Hubble's 2.4 meters and even Herschel's 3.5 meters mirrors. Can you imagine what wonderful perspectives could be opened up by this mighty machine?

There are still research areas where optical telescopes have significant advantages and one of the most interesting is the search for the ninth planet of the Solar System, also called Planet X. Scientists suggested the existence of this planet when they tried to explain eccentric orbits of a few tiny objects observed on the outskirts of the Solar System. It was as if their trajectories were aligned by the gravity of a much larger object. Some theoretical models suggested that the planet had to be somewhere between two and 15 times bigger than Earth and its orbit might lie somewhere between 250 and 1500 Astronomical Units from the Sun. One Astronomical Unit is the average distance between Earth and the Sun. At the moment we have no idea what kind of world it could be; based on its extremely far distance from the Sun, it is expected to be a very cold and dark place. Our beloved star may look like just one of many bright stars in Planet X's sky. By the way, the low temperature of Planet X is the reason why advanced infrared telescopes may struggle to find elusive Planet X.

Today, the hunters for Planet X patiently scour the sky using survey telescopes similar to Japan's Subaru telescope on Mauna Kea volcano on the island of Hawaii. However, the fast-approaching completion of the Rubin Observatory Summit Facility located on the Cerro Pachón ridge in north-central Chile promises a remarkable boost in the data collection rate. Whereas for most telescopes it would take months or years to survey the whole sky, Rubin observatory will do it in just three nights. Once a glimpse of Planet X is detected by a survey telescope and its location revealed, then the precious time of the most advanced optical telescopes could be spent studying the mysterious object.

My two optical super telescopes of choice are the Very Large Telescope array on Cerro Paranal in the Atacama Desert of northern Chile and the Thirty Meter Telescope, which is being built on Mauna Kea, Hawaii.

The Very Large Telescope array, operated by the European Southern Observatory, consists of four Unit Telescopes with main mirrors of 8.2m diameter and four movable 1.8m diameter Auxiliary Telescopes, which are generally used separately but can be synchronised to achieve an extremely high angular resolution that allows to distinguish the two headlights of a car at a distance of the Moon. The first of the Unit Telescopes was commissioned in 1999. Today, all eight telescopes are operational.

The Thirty Meter Telescope would become the largest visible-light telescope based on the Earth's terrain, but its building was delayed because of its planned location on Mauna Kea, the most sacred mountain in Native Hawaiian culture. After a long legal battle, the construction resumed in July 2019. The centrepiece of the TMT Observatory is going to be a Ritchey-Chrétien telescope with a 30m diameter primary mirror that will have nine times more area than the largest currently existing visible-light telescope in the world. That will make possible observations of planets, moons, and small bodies like planetoids, comets and asteroids in the Solar System with unprecedented image resolution, more than 12 times sharper than those obtained from the Hubble Space Telescope. Ultimately, the far superior capabilities of the Thirty Meter Telescope could open up areas of science impossible to envisage today.

ACKNOWLEDGEMENTS

A debt of gratitude: to my soulmates and first readers Oksana and Marsha. Without you it would just not be possible.

To wonderful Alice Kouzmenko, who transformed a string of words into a readable text.

To the gifted artist Marina Salihova for amazing illustrations.

And finally to all my friends and colleagues for inspirational conversations and sharing with me their knowledge and ideas.

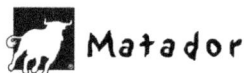

For exclusive discounts on Matador titles,
sign up to our occasional newsletter at
troubador.co.uk/bookshop